"You Won't Need To Worry About That In Future."

Her breath stalled. "What do you mean?"

"We're getting married."

"Married?" She heard the words and thought she might faint. The minute he'd learned about their child, she'd thought it might come to this, but hearing it out loud hit her hard.

And yet…if she had her son, she had everything that mattered. "So you're *not* going to try and take Nathan from me?" she said weakly.

"No." He paused. "Of course, if you don't marry me, I'll fight for custody. A child should have both parents. Even if we don't love each other."

Dear Reader,

Do you believe in love at first sight? How does someone know in an instant that they will love the other person for the rest of their life? And what if something happens and love turns to hate? I imagine it would be almost impossible to trust in your feelings ever again after that.

My heroine, Gemma Watkins, thought she'd found true love from the moment she met Tate Chandler—until he accused her of something she didn't do. As for Tate, he hadn't planned on "ever after" when he first met Gemma. He was only interested in an affair—until she betrayed him with his best friend. Gemma may have been in love, and Tate in lust, but both of them went from thinking they knew the other, to realizing they couldn't rely on their own judgment at all.

And now there's a child involved, and Gemma and Tate have to put aside their differences and concentrate on what's important. Will the love for their son show their real characters to each other?

True love is exactly that—true forever. Nothing pulls it apart. This time Gemma and Tate have the chance to change their future together, but only by rising above their past.

Happy reading!

Maxine

MAXINE SULLIVAN

SECRET SON, CONVENIENT WIFE

Recycling programs
for this product may
not exist in your area.

ISBN-13: 978-0-373-73098-8

SECRET SON, CONVENIENT WIFE

Copyright © 2011 by Maxine Sullivan

www.Harlequin.com

Printed in U.S.A.

Books by Maxine Sullivan

Desire

*Australian Millionaires

MAXINE SULLIVAN

This *USA TODAY* bestselling author credits her mother for her lifelong love of romance novels, so it was a natural extension for Maxine to want to write her own romances. She thinks there's nothing better than being a writer and is thrilled to be one of the few Australians to write for the Desire line.

Maxine lives in Melbourne, Australia, but over the years has traveled to New Zealand, the U.K. and the U.S.A. In her own backyard, her husband's job ensured they saw the diversity of the countryside, from the tropics to the Outback, country towns to the cities. She is married to Geoff, who has proven his hero status many times over the years. They have two handsome sons and an assortment of much-loved, previously abandoned animals.

Maxine would love to hear from you. She can be contacted through her website at www.maxinesullivan.com.

To Elvina Payet, and Bec and Scott Schulz for their support and helpful advice with this book. Thanks guys!

One

Gemma Watkins stopped dead as she stepped outside the hospital waiting room. A tall man was striding toward her along the corridor. His broad shoulders, his purposeful walk, reminded her of…

Please God, not Tate Chandler!

In that instant he saw her. His footsteps faltered just a hint, then increased pace until he reached her. "Gemma," he rasped.

His voice traveled under her skin like a shiver of apprehension. This was the man who'd once been her lover. The man she'd once fallen in love with. The man who'd cut out her heart almost two years ago.

She couldn't believe it was him. Tate Chandler was an Australian who'd taken his family's luxury watchmaking business to new levels and high international standing. He was a man suited to his surroundings, whether it was here in this large hospital close to the city, his well-appointed headquarters on the most prestigious street in Melbourne or his luxurious penthouse in one of the city's most affluent suburbs. He was a billionaire with a powerful presence that went beyond his supreme good looks. He had the golden touch…and his touch was golden. *She* knew that firsthand.

Gemma swallowed the panic in her throat. "Hello, Tate."

His blue eyes flicked over her blond hair tumbling to her shoulders, to the flush of her cheeks, as if he couldn't quite help himself, then as quickly his eyes narrowed. "I hope your being here is merely a coincidence."

It took a moment to actually absorb the words. Her brows drew together. "I'm not sure what you mean."

Skepticism crossed his face. "My family dedicated the new children's wing in my grandfather's name today. Surely you saw mention of it? It's been in all the media."

"No, I didn't." She'd been too busy working and trying to keep her head above water. "So your grandfather's… dead?"

"Three months ago."

"I'm sorry." Tate had been very close to him. "But you can't think I came here today to see *you*. I could see you anytime I like."

His lips twisted. "You think so?"

Her heart constricted. He hadn't forgiven her for what he saw as her betrayal. Had she expected he would?

And that brought her back to why she was at the hospital today. What bad luck that she'd decided just now to look for the nurse from the recovery room. She supposed she could be grateful that the rest of his family didn't appear to be anywhere in sight. "Well, I must—"

"What are you doing here then?"

She saw not one ounce of kindness in his eyes. "I'm with a…friend."

"Male?"

"Er…yes."

"Of course it's a male," he mocked. "Nothing's changed there, has it?"

Her hesitation made her look guilty, but he couldn't know it wasn't for the reason he thought. Realizing this was her "out," she lifted her chin. "This has nothing to do with you, Tate. Goodbye." She went to move past him, but he put his hand on her arm, stopping her.

"Does the poor sucker know he's one of many?"

"I—"

"You what? Don't care? Believe me, *I* know that more than anyone."

The words stung. She'd willingly given herself to Tate the day she'd met him at a party held by her architect boss. At the time, she'd wished she hadn't given away her virginity years ago to a boyfriend in high school. She'd fallen instantly in love with Tate and had known then what her mother had meant when she'd advised Gemma to keep herself for the man she loved. Gemma would have been proud for Tate to have been her first.

She could only thank the Lord now that she hadn't told Tate she loved him. Somehow she'd kept that secret to herself and had managed to keep some of her pride intact when he'd turned his back on her after a month-long affair. During their short weeks together, they'd barely left Tate's penthouse apartment. His best friend had been the only one to know about their relationship.

The memory of it all made her shudder. Their unexpected reunion today was so unfair, yet she couldn't tell Tate the truth. Not now. He might decide to—

"Oh, there you are, Gemma." A female voice a few

feet away from them made Gemma suck in a quick, sharp breath. She turned to look at the nurse from the recovery room. Oh, God, she'd almost forgotten.

"He's fine, love," Deirdre said before Gemma could ask. "And out of recovery now."

"Thank God!" Gemma forgot about Tate as intense relief washed over her. They'd said it would be a minor operation, but there were always risks with these things.

Deirdre's gaze dropped to Tate's hand on Gemma's arm, and she frowned slightly. Gemma knew she had to act quickly. From the depths of her being, she dragged up a reassuring smile. She didn't want any issues here. The sooner she got away from Tate, the better. "I'm coming now, Deirdre. Thank you."

The nurse paused a second longer, before seeming to accept there wasn't a problem. "I'll go tell Nathan that Mommy's coming then." She headed back to the recovery room.

Gemma didn't need Tate's tightening grip to feel the increased tension emanating from him. Her heartbeat thudded in her ears as she gathered the nerve to look into his eyes, torn between running to Nathan and staying here and standing guard.

"You have a *son?*"

Her heart quailed. How could she deny it now? "Yes."

His head went back, as if from a blow. Then, without warning, his expression changed, turned suspicious. "And his name is Nathan?"

She gave a quick nod.

"My grandfather's name was Nathaniel."

"It's a common enough name," she said, finding her voice, kicking herself now for allowing herself that one weakness.

All at once, he swore. Then he dropped her arm and strode past her.

Like a mother bear, Gemma jumped in front of him, putting herself between him and her son. "He's only ten months old, Tate," she lied.

He stopped. "He's not Drake's, is he?"

"No!" He'd never believed her innocent where his best friend had been concerned. Drake Fulton had made her uneasy, always being too friendly whenever Tate left them alone together, making it more than clear he wanted her. In the end he hadn't gotten her, but he'd made damn sure Tate hadn't held on to her either.

"So your son belongs to another man."

She dropped her hand. "Yes."

Him.

She prayed Tate would turn and walk away. Instead, he surprised her and moved ahead. She quickly caught up to him, frantic with worry. "Wh-where are you going?"

He continued toward the recovery room, purpose in every step. "You've lied to me before."

"I didn't. I—" She sidestepped a young couple walking down the middle of the corridor, then caught up to him again.

He ignored her as he hit a button outside the recovery room to open the electronic doors. She went with him as he entered the room, watched his gaze slice down the row of occupied beds. Past Deirdre now attending to one of the patients…past the nurse at her station…until he came to the crib set slightly away from the rest of the beds.

Time was suspended in the air.

Then, almost in sync, they both started forward, stopping only when they reached the small blond boy playing with his teddy bear. Nathan looked up, and Gemma held her breath.

Tate couldn't know.

He just couldn't…

And then Tate turned to look at her, his face white. His eyes skinned her alive.

She was going to pay dearly for this.

Tate felt the blood drain from his face the minute the infant looked up and caught him by the heart. Caught and grabbed and would never let go.

For just a moment, Tate almost wished that the boy *wasn't* his, that he could turn and walk away and never have to see Gemma again. He didn't want her in his life again.

But one look and he knew.

This was his *son*.

And Tate wasn't going anywhere.

Just then, the boy saw his mother. He dropped his teddy bear and threw his arms out to her with a cry, and Gemma gave a small sob as she ran to the crib and lifted him up and over the side. "Sh, darling, Mommy's here," she murmured, hugging him and soothing him.

Mommy.

Daddy.

His.

She leaned back to check the boy. It would have been touching if Tate hadn't suddenly realized something.

"What's wrong with him?" he heard himself ask in a croaky voice, not sure if he could bear knowing.

Gemma lifted her head—and her chin. "What do you mean? He's perfect."

She'd taken his comment the wrong way. He'd have been offended if he'd had the time. "I'm talking about why he's here in the hospital." The child didn't show any outward signs of an operation except for the hospital gown.

She winced. "Yes, of course." Then she took a breath. "They put tiny tubes inside his ears to drain them. He was getting repeated ear infections and the antibiotics weren't working anymore. Without the tubes, he could suffer hearing loss, and that could affect his speech and development."

As serious as that sounded, Tate felt the tension ease out of him. Thank God it wasn't anything critical.

And then he remembered her lies, and the tension was back. "You didn't think to tell me about it?" he said, keeping his voice low, aware of others in the room.

"Why would I?"

"Because he's mine, dammit."

Her arms tightened around her son. "No, he isn't."

"Don't lie, Gemma. He has my eyes."

Fear came and went on her face. "No, he's got blond hair like me. He *looks* like me. He doesn't look like you at all. And he's only ten months old."

Nathan *did* look like her—except for the eyes. "He's mine. And he's a year old. I know it, and so do you."

"Tate, please," she choked out. "I don't think this is the right time or place to discuss this."

"Gemma…" He had to know this minute. He had to be sure.

She shuddered, then expelled a deep breath. "Yes, he's yours."

Hearing the words out loud was like a wave breaking over Tate. For a moment he couldn't breathe, couldn't get his bearings. And then he looked at his son. He wanted to hold him in his arms and *feel* the moment, but as much as he wanted to hug Nathan tight, Tate figured things had to be taken slowly. A child had the right to personal space.

Gemma looked dismayed. "Wh-what are you going to do now?"

He had to concentrate, and that was hard when he was so damn angry with her. "We'll have a paternity test done first. As proof."

Her eyes widened. "So you're not really sure?"

"I'm sure, but I want there to be absolutely no doubt about this. Besides, it wouldn't be the first time I've been fooled by you, would it?"

He would never forget finding her kissing his best friend. And then having Drake awkwardly confess she'd been coming on to him from the start. The incident had made Tate want to kill both of them. Much to his credit, Drake had been honorable enough not to let her seduce him. It was the measure of the man that he could withstand such a beautiful woman. Sure, out in the corridor Tate had asked her if the infant was Drake's, but the question had been more about covering all bases than believing his friend had slept with her. Drake wouldn't do that. He always kept his word.

Unlike Gemma.

"I've all but admitted he's your son, Tate. There's no need for a paternity test."

"Your word isn't good enough, I'm afraid." His jaw felt so tight he thought it would snap. "We'll talk about everything later."

She straightened. "No, it'll have to wait. I'm taking Nathan home as soon as the doctor releases him."

"We'll be going to my home."

She gasped. "There's no need for that."

"Isn't there?"

She swallowed. "He's already unsettled from being here. I want to get him back in familiar surroundings. He needs the comfort of his own home right now."

Only for his son's sake did Tate relent. "Then I'm

coming with you and staying the night, but tomorrow we'll be going to my place."

"What!"

"Don't worry. I'll sleep on your sofa. We need to talk, and I'm not letting you out of my sight."

"Can't we leave it until tomorrow? It's only just lunchtime. I'm sure you want to return to your office and get some work done today."

"No."

That's all he was going to say. He'd already missed the first year of his son's life, he wasn't missing a minute more. Having his child without telling him was unforgivable. What if something had gone wrong with the operation? What if he'd never gotten to stand here with his own flesh and blood? What if Nathan had needed *him?* Tate's chest constricted with the oddest pain.

Right then the nurse appeared beside them. "Didn't I tell you your baby boy would be fine?" she teased Gemma.

Gemma nodded. "Thank you, Deirdre. You've been wonderful."

"You're very welcome, love," the nurse said. "Now, I see the doctor has just come in, so you should be able to take your little one home shortly."

The younger man appeared at Deirdre's side and glanced from Tate to Nathan, then back to Tate. "So you're the father," he said without question.

Gemma made a sound that could be mistaken for a sob, but all Tate felt was fatherly pride swelling up inside his chest. The doctor's assumption was based solely on the sight of Tate and Nathan together.

Father and son.

Tate cleared his throat. "Yes, I'm Nathan's father."

The doctor accepted that, then turned his attention to the infant.

Tate sent Gemma a look that said it all: There was no going back now.

Two

"Look straight ahead and keep walking to the limousine." Tate's hand slipped around her waist as if he were shielding her from the man standing in the parking lot. Or shielding his son was more likely, she thought, trying to ignore the protective feel of this man beside her as she carried Nathan.

"Who is he?"

"A photographer. He was here for the dedication. I'm not sure why he's still here. Probably just our bad luck he was leaving at the same time as us."

The open car door loomed ahead, and it was sheer instinct that orchestrated their haste onto the backseat in a matter of moments. Then the driver came around and Tate pressed a button to lower the screen as the older man slid in behind the steering wheel. "Go straight home, Clive, but take it easy." He was clearly thinking about Nathan, who now sat between them in the car seat the driver had moved from her car. The screen came back up.

Gemma finished checking that her son was comfortable and had his teddy bear, then she looked up. "I want to go to *my* home, Tate."

"And lead the media straight to you and Nathan?"

"It was only one guy, and he can't know anything," she said, trying not to overreact. "You said earlier you would take me home and have someone collect my car. I'm sure you want to get back to the office. You can come over tonight and we'll talk then." She needed some time to herself to sort things out in her head.

He snorted. "And find you and Nathan gone when I return?"

She blinked. "Where would we go?"

"Your parents' place, for a start."

"You'd find me in next to no time." Not that she would go there. Or even *could*. Her middle-class parents had cut her out of their staid and virtuous lives, but she couldn't tell him that. Apart from it hurting too much, she wouldn't give him that power over her.

And she had no other relatives to whom she could turn. With her parents starting a new life and coming to Australia from England straight after their marriage many years ago, distant relatives were exactly that. Distant.

He picked up his cell phone and began speaking to someone called Peggy, who by the sound of his instructions was the housekeeper. His last housekeeper had been an older lady who'd merely come in to clean the apartment a few times a week, usually during the day when no one was there.

Accepting that she couldn't change anything right now, Gemma tuned him out. Lord, she was still reeling from everything that had happened today, and in her life in general over the past two years. She didn't regret having Nathan—not at all—but her life had changed so much since meeting Tate.

Not wanting Tate to learn she was having his baby, she'd left her job in an architect's office, downsized her trendy city flat and moved into a one-bedroom apartment in the suburbs. But getting to and from work in the city would have become impossible once she'd had Nathan, so she'd taken a job closer to home. At least then she hadn't had to worry about the hour of traveling each way cutting into quality time with her child.

She'd done her best, and it *had* been good enough, but it still hadn't been easy to stop herself from running to Tate and asking him to take them away from it all. She'd been more afraid he would only take Nathan away from *her*. Tate had kicked her out of his life once before. She had no doubt that if he believed he was doing the right thing, he would kick her out again—and keep her son.

Yet all this heartache could have been avoided if only Tate had believed her eighteen months ago. He'd given a party for his best friend's birthday and invited her to play hostess. She'd been so excited. Later in the evening, she'd written a note to Tate, telling him to meet her in his study for a kiss, and asked the waiter to give it to him.

The room had been dark when he stepped inside and she'd thrown herself at him. Only...it wasn't Tate. The real Tate had opened the door and caught her kissing his best friend thoroughly, her arms around Drake's neck. It seemed Drake had followed her into the room, but it had been *she* who looked guilty.

The thought of that night made her feel ill, so she pushed it out of her mind, and a while later the limousine turned into a driveway. A security guard opened two large gates, showcasing a beautiful mansion. Gemma said the first thing that came to mind. "This isn't your apartment."

"It's my home now."

A spasm went through her heart. This was more than big enough for a family. "Were you planning on marrying?"

"One day."

"So there's someone special in your life?"

"Only my son."

She looked away, thankful the car was pulling to a stop. The pain of losing Tate had been made worse by frequently seeing him in the papers with a beautiful woman on his arm. Not that it was any of her business, but knowing he wasn't serious about anyone made her feel better about things.

Everything was a bit of a blur after they left the car. Gemma insisted on carrying Nathan again as they went inside. He was usually a happy child, but his eyes were wide and she could sense he was confused by everything today.

He wasn't the only one!

Tate briefly introduced them to the housekeeper, who beamed at them both. "He's beautiful, Mr. Chandler."

Tate's face softened as he looked at his son. "Yes, he is, Peggy." Then he glanced at Gemma and his eyes hardened before he turned back to Peggy. "So the suite next to mine is ready?"

"Of course." She hesitated. "Mr. Chandler…I was thinking. I have a crib you can use temporarily. It's not an expensive one, but Clive and I keep it in our rooms for when we mind the grandchildren. He could set it up in the suite…until you get your own, that is. We won't need it anytime soon."

Tate nodded. "Good idea, Peggy. Thank you for thinking of it."

Peggy's face filled with pleasure. "You're welcome. I'll get Clive right on it."

Tate put his hand under Gemma's elbow and herded her toward the staircase. "Good. I'll talk to you shortly about what else we need."

Of course Tate would give her and Nathan their own suite, Gemma thought with relief. Tate hadn't wanted her once he'd "discovered" her with Drake. He wouldn't want her now.

As he opened the bedroom door, he indicated his own rooms farther along the landing. The distance was considerable, thank goodness.

Her suite was bigger than her apartment. The large bedroom had a king-sized bed, a sitting room and a gold-encrusted ensuite. It was as one would expect in such a house, except that while the bedroom was suitable for a crawling infant the sitting room definitely wasn't childproof.

"I might need to move a few things out of Nathan's way. And that couch might need a cover." It looked like it was made of velvet. Not exactly safe for grubby little fingers.

"I don't care about the furniture, but I don't want him hurting himself, so do what you need to do. I'll make sure Peggy has everything else in the house childproofed as soon as possible." Tate put the bag of baby paraphernalia she'd brought to the hospital on one of the chairs. "Does he need anything heated up?"

"No. This is fine." Gemma had a bottle of juice in the baby bag. "He'll probably take a nap." He'd been sleepy in the car, though now he squirmed to be put down.

Gemma placed Nathan on the plush carpet with his teddy bear, then closed the sitting room door so he couldn't go in there. He wasn't quite walking yet, but he could crawl like the wind and at least she could keep a firm eye on him in here.

"Clive will bring the crib up, and I'll be back soon. Peggy will need a list of anything Nathan needs. We'll order a crib and other things tomorrow. I want them as soon as possible."

How wonderful to be able to snap your fingers and have things happen. She'd snap her fingers and get her and Nathan out of here if she could. "I've got everything he needs at home."

Arrogance bounced off him. "I intend my son to have the best."

"He has. He's got *me*."

"Of course. And now you won't need to worry about anything else."

Her breath stalled. "What do you mean?"

"We're getting married."

"Ma-married?" She heard the words and thought she might faint. The minute he'd learned about Nathan, she'd known he was old-fashioned enough to insist on marriage, but hearing it out loud hit her hard.

And yet…if she had her son, she had everything that mattered. "So you're *not* going to try and take Nathan from me?"

"No." He allowed a silence. "Of course, if you don't marry me I'll fight for custody. A child should have both parents."

She quickly pulled herself together. To live with the man she'd once loved, knowing he believed she'd cheated on him—wouldn't her life be a living hell? How would that affect Nathan? Perhaps if she pointed this out…

"Even if we don't love each other?"

"Yes."

"Even if you consider me a liar?"

"Yes."

"That won't be a marriage, Tate. That'll be a nightmare, not only for us but for Nathan."

His mouth tightened. "If you care about your son, you'll make it work."

"That's unfair."

"Is it?"

"Perhaps part-time custody," she began, knowing she was in a losing battle now, not even sure why she didn't simply give in. Tate always won.

"No."

"Hear me out. I—"

Just then, the infant babbled something. When she looked, Nathan had pulled himself up by the side of the bed and was hanging on to the quilt, the cheesiest of grins telling them how clever he thought he was. Gemma's heart overflowed with love.

Then something about Tate made her look at him. In his eyes was twelve months' worth of longing for a son he'd never known. "Tate, I—"

"Don't, Gemma," he said tersely. "Don't say another word." He twisted on his heels and left the room.

Tate stood at the living room window, a hard knot in the center of his chest. He still felt shell-shocked by today's events, like he was in a war zone with everything raining down on him.

And then his infant son had smiled and lit up the room, and Tate knew there was a reason he had run into Gemma today. His son might have a mother, but Nathan needed his father. Tate had never felt more certain of anything in his life.

God, how could Gemma have kept Nathan from him? And how could she let him believe—even briefly—that she'd had another man's child? He'd felt physically ill in that hospital corridor. The reminder of her with other men, the shock of thinking she'd had another man's baby, had knocked the breath from his body.

There had only been two times in his life when he'd been this winded. Once when he'd caught Gemma kissing Drake, and the other when he was twelve and his mother had left his father for another man.

Darlene Chandler had supposedly gone away on a trip to visit a sick cousin, but Tate had overheard his father talking to her on the phone. Never would Tate have thought he'd hear his tall, strong father pleading for his wife to come back to him. Nothing had worked, and Jonathan Chandler had seemed to shrink in size, as if he'd lost a part of himself. Not even Tate's young sister, Bree, who'd been too young to know and who was the apple of her father's eye, could get through to him.

A week later, his mother had walked back in the door.

Tate had always felt protective of his father after that. He loved his mother, and somehow his parents' marriage had been better than before, but Tate couldn't forget how loving a woman could tear a man down. He was determined never to let that happen to *him*.

Certainly not with Gemma.

It had been all about sex with them, nothing more. He'd never wanted a woman like he'd wanted her. From the moment he'd set eyes on Gemma, he'd needed her with an ache that had gone right through him. He'd spent every spare second of the next month trying to ease that ache. She hadn't moved into his penthouse, exactly, but they'd spent so much time there, she might as well have.

He'd been confident their affair would eventually run its course. He wasn't fool enough to believe it had been about love. He'd known he'd never give his heart to any woman.

Sure, one day he'd marry, and he'd have kids, but that was in the future. Until then, he thought, he had plenty of time to tire of Gemma and then go back to playing the field.

He just hadn't expected *Gemma* to be the one playing games, and definitely not with his best friend. She may not have slept with Drake, but it hadn't been for want of trying.

Memories flooded back. It had been Drake's birthday, and Tate had asked Gemma if she'd host the party. No wonder she'd agreed so enthusiastically. He'd thought it was because she was finally meeting more of his friends. In reality it was because she'd planned on seducing Drake.

God, he'd been a fool. She'd used him two years ago, making him think she was a woman to be trusted. How could he still want a woman like her? Sure, she was very beautiful, even with those small lines of tiredness under her eyes and a weariness to her shoulders that could not be manufactured. But she would milk his sympathy for all its worth.

He was one step ahead of her this time.

He'd been duped once by her charm. He wouldn't let that happen again.

After Clive delivered the crib and Peggy brought up a tray with a plate of daintily cut sandwiches and a pot of coffee with two cups, Gemma thanked them and settled Nathan down for a nap. In the sitting room and alone at last, she gratefully poured herself a coffee and sat on the couch, not realizing until then how desperate she was to ease the dryness in her mouth. The sandwiches she left untouched. She couldn't eat a thing right now.

As she wrapped her cold hands around the china cup, it was hard to believe how things had spiraled so out of control within a few hours. God, why had she chosen to get involved with Tate Chandler in the first place? Why couldn't she have settled for a simple man? Damn him for being a man of substance in more ways than one. Moneyed or poor, he'd fight to have his son. Of course, that left her with no options at all.

Just then, there was a soft rap on the bedroom door. She hurried to answer it, knowing Tate was being quiet for Nathan's sake. His manner reminded her of how a lover might sneak into her room. But that was crazy thinking. Tate had never snuck into her room or her apartment. He hadn't needed to.

Tate's eyes flickered to his son in the crib then back to her as he stepped inside the door. "Everything okay?"

He meant his son.

"Yes. Coffee?" Not waiting for an answer, she led the way to the sitting room, quietly closing the connecting door. All at once, she was aware of Tate behind her, following her, feeling his eyes on her as he stood and watched her pour.

She handed the cup to him, then gestured to the other chair, giving the impression that this was her territory. At least it made her feel she had the upper hand in here.

That impression didn't last long.

Not with Tate.

He didn't sit. He drained the coffee from the small cup, then went to the window and stood looking out, his back totally immovable and unbending. "By the way, you won't be getting your car."

She'd been about to put down her cup, but her hand stopped midair. "What do you mean?"

He slowly turned around. "They couldn't even start it, let alone drive it out of the hospital grounds. I've told Clive to get rid of it."

The coffee cup wobbled and she almost dropped it onto the saucer. "What!" she exclaimed, keeping her voice low so as not to wake her son. "You had no right to do that."

"You're not driving my son around in that thing."

She ignored the fact that he didn't care that *she* drove around in it. "My car is only five years old. Admittedly, sometimes it can be temperamental in starting, but apart from that it works fine." It had been a good buy at a time when she'd needed to be very careful with money. She *still* needed to be careful with money. "Anyway, I need my car to get to work."

An arrogant brow lifted. "You work?"

"Yes, that's how we mere mortals pay our bills," she snapped sarcastically.

"If you'd told me about Nathan in the first place, you wouldn't need to worry about the bills."

"And then I'd have bigger problems, wouldn't I?"

"You've got them now."

"Damn you, Tate."

There was a moment of stony silence.

"Why didn't you tell me about Nathan?" he demanded, his voice tight with strain.

"I had my reasons."

"You took it upon yourself to keep my son from me. Those reasons had better be bloody good."

There was no way she'd let him see how heartbroken she still was by everything that had happened between them or he'd use it against her. "You already thought the worst of me. I had nothing else to lose by keeping him to myself."

His eyes narrowed. "So this is about you not wanting to share him with me?"

It wasn't that. She would have been glad to share with him, only she wasn't convinced Tate would want to share with *her*. "At least I only had to please myself," she said offhandedly.

His mouth tightened. "He needed both of us, Gemma. He still needs both of us."

"We did all right without you."

Anger flashed in his eyes. "Really?"

She wondered if somehow he knew about her struggle to put food on the table—not for her son but for herself. But then, how could he possibly know that? Was he talking about her car?

Anyway, she'd made sure Nathan had everything he needed, the most important thing being love. Tate may have killed her love for him when he kicked her out, but she'd never had reservations about her love for his baby.

"Tate, think about this. If we marry, do you really want your son living in such a stressful environment? Because it can't be anything but. You know it and I know it."

"He doesn't seem too stressed out right now," he said, directing her gaze to the quiet coming from the bedroom.

"That's probably the anesthetic. It may not have worn off." And she couldn't help but add, "Look, I have no doubt all the attention he'll get from you will be a novelty to him at first, but it can't last. There's more to being a father than claiming a child as your own."

"You say that when you haven't even given me a chance?"

"You were quick to drop *me* like a hot rock," she said, surprised by how cool she sounded.

"The two things don't compare," he said dismissively. "And actually the shoe is on the other foot. I'd say you're the person least likely to stick with parenthood."

That stung. "I'm a very good mother."

"And I'll be a very good father."

Stalemate.

"Who looks after Nathan while you're at work?" he fired at her.

"He goes to a day-care center. And it's a very good one," she said defensively. "I wouldn't leave him there otherwise."

"And the job? I ran into your old boss ages ago, and he told me you'd left."

Clearly he must not have been interested enough to ask where she'd gone. Why did that hurt now? "I work for a courier company. In the dispatch department."

"A bit of a comedown, isn't it?"

"There's nothing wrong with working in a demanding environment. We all work very hard."

"I wasn't denigrating the courier business."

Her top lip curled. "No, just me."

His look said he acknowledged that. "As my wife, you don't have to work."

"I won't leave them in the lurch," she said, then could have kicked herself. She didn't want to hint that she was prepared to give in to another of his decrees.

"I don't think you've thought it through, Gemma. There are plenty of people looking for work, and some of them might not like a rich man's wife taking a job that someone else needs. Would you be comfortable with that?"

She sent him a sour look. Why was nothing going her way today? He was right, damn him. If she kept working there, word might get out, then how would it look to work friends who struggled to keep their jobs and food on the table for their families? And now that she didn't have a car, she could just imagine rolling up in Tate's limo each day.

"Wouldn't you rather stay home with Nathan?" Tate asked more quietly.

There was nothing for it but to admit, "Okay, yes. I miss being with him." She missed every minute she was away from her son. She'd hated leaving him, even knowing it was good for him to be around other people and that he was in good hands.

"There you are then. Problem solved." Tate had a results-driven mind set in everything he did. Nothing had changed there.

"It's all black and white to you, isn't it? There are no shades of gray. No room for error."

"Things are what they are. For now, take the time off to stay home with Nathan and we'll worry about the future later. He needs his mother, and you look like you could do with a long rest from performing two jobs."

Inwardly, she slumped with an odd relief, knowing the one good thing about marrying Tate would be getting help. She was so tired. She'd been responsible for everything, with no one to turn to for so long. There had been the trauma of breaking up with him, then the realization she was pregnant, the acceptance that her parents would be no help. Then she'd had to move to somewhere less expensive, find a new local job that would give her time off to have the baby—all without any real break for herself. She'd do it all again, for her son, but it would be nice to lean on someone else for a change—until she could get back to normal.

"At least I know you didn't deliberately get pregnant," he said, surprising her with the backhanded compliment just as she'd started to relax.

"I could have put a pin in one of the condoms," she quipped, wanting to rock him.

His eyes lasered on to her. "Did you?"

She blinked. "Of course not. Anyway, why would I?"

"Seems clear to me." He looked around the room. "You had a lot to gain."

She was offended by the suggestion. "I don't believe I've asked anything of you. In fact, I don't *want* anything from you. Not a damn thing."

He regarded her, his expression one of mockery. "You know, I look at you and wonder how I could have been such a fool." His gaze slid down, then up. "Of course, you *do* have a great body, and you can certainly charm a man right out of his pants." He paused just enough to be insulting. "But you know that already, don't you? You don't need me to remind you how quickly I took you to my bed…and how quickly you let me."

All at once she knew she was fighting for something more than her son. She wasn't sure what. Perhaps the right to be judged fairly and honestly.

"Tate, no matter what has happened between us in the past, I don't—and can't—regret having Nathan." She angled her chin in defiance. "So do your worst…but do it to *me*."

A dash of admiration entered the depths of his eyes, but a sudden knock at the sitting room door stole it away.

Tate opened the door.

The housekeeper stood there. "Mr. Chandler, there's a phone call for you. It's your father. He says it's urgent."

Tate seemed to stiffen. He turned to Gemma and nodded, before stepping out in the corridor and closing the door behind him. She sagged against the sofa, glad he'd gone. She needed the breathing space…needed *not* to think. Lord, it had been such a long day.

Tate was back too soon.

This time he didn't bother to knock.

And this time his face seemed to be carved from stone.

"What's the matter?" she asked.

"The hospital announced a few weeks ago that my family's going to be the recipient of a humanitarian award. It's for our support of the hospital, especially the children's wing, over the years."

"That's very nice." She didn't have it in her to be enthusiastic right now. She had too much on her mind.

He didn't look happy. "One of the newspapers just called my father. They wanted to know how he feels about being a grandfather." He paused. "They know about Nathan."

"Wh-what?"

"Dammit, Gemma, they wanted to know why I turned my back on my son."

"No!"

"What else would you think they'd make of it?" He shot her a suddenly suspicious look. "Did you tell that nurse anything about us before you left the hospital? It seems strange that a photographer waited for us long after the ceremony ended."

She gasped. "I didn't! Why would I?"

"You knew I wouldn't walk away from my son. Perhaps you thought you could get the public on your side, so they'd think I'm a rotten father. That way, if you tell them what a terrible person I am, you might win any future custody battle."

"No!" She was appalled he'd think she'd do something like that. She'd never do it to Nathan. One day he'd grow up, and she wanted him to respect his father, despite how she felt about Tate personally. "My son is not a commodity to be used like that."

He held her gaze. "I'm glad to hear you say that about *our* son." His brow knitted together. "It must have been someone from the hospital."

He believed her? She wanted to cry with relief.

She forced herself to think. "I can't see it being Deirdre. She was too professional. And the doctor didn't seem to recognize you." She tried to remember everything from the moment she'd run into Tate. "There were plenty of other people in the recovery room. Any one of them could have put two and two together." With the crib being away from the others, Gemma suspected she and Tate had been out of hearing range. "Our body language would have been enough to show something was up."

"True." He expelled a breath. "Dammit, if one newspaper knows, you can bet the rest will, too. It'll crush my grandmother if the hospital decides not to give the award. She and my grandfather worked hard to support them and my parents carried on the tradition."

"Would they really do that? Take it away from your family, that is."

He arched a cynical brow. "My family receives a humanitarian award, yet it looks like we can't even be responsible for a child of ours? What do you think?"

He was right.

"Bloody hell, the timing couldn't be worse."

Her chin came up of its own accord. "I'm sorry if you feel *our* son is an inconvenience."

"That's not what I meant, and you know it." He ran his fingers through his hair, for the first time looking really upset.

It was such an unusual sight that Gemma felt an unwelcome surge of sympathy. "Perhaps you could appeal to the board's better nature?" she asked, but she knew it was a silly suggestion the minute the words left her mouth.

"Do they have one?" he quipped, though his sarcasm wasn't directed at her. "No, as much as I hate to give in to them, I'll have to make a statement acknowledging Nathan as my son and telling them we're getting married as soon as possible."

"But we were getting married for Nathan's sake anyway," she pointed out.

"Yes, but now we're going to put on a real show. I don't want a scandal following our son all his life," he said, his voice low and rough.

Her heart filled with warmth to know he had a vested interest in Nathan's well-being. "What sort of show?"

"We'll say we had a misunderstanding that's been righted, and we'll show them how much in love we are." He paused. "I'm sure you'll have no trouble playing your part. You did it once before, remember? You totally hoodwinked me. I'm sure you can do it again for everyone else."

So it was back to this.

She lifted her head high with dignity. She'd just about had enough. "Please leave."

Clearly no one had ever said that to him before. A muscle flexed in his jaw, then he swung around and grabbed the door handle. "My parents will be here within the hour. They want to meet their grandson."

He was gone.

Their grandson, he'd said.

They didn't want to meet *her.*

Gemma stood there feeling insignificant and small—a nobody who amounted to nothing in the lives of the family she was soon to marry into.

Welcome to the world of the Chandlers.

Three

Ten days later, Tate stood at the end of the red carpet in his family's country estate north of Melbourne and watched a vision descend the sweeping staircase into the old ballroom. He heard the guests' gasps of delight, and pride swelled inside him. Gemma looked so beautiful and elegant, her strapless white wedding gown cascading down to the ground. If he *had* been in love with her, he would have had a lump in his throat right about now. Under the right circumstances, he would have been happy to have her as his wife.

God, this woman certainly knew how to make a grand entrance, even at her own wedding. Was it intentional? Probably. Yet he saw her hand slightly gripping the banister. Perhaps she wasn't as self-assured as she wanted to appear. Nothing was ever as it seemed with Gemma.

Like right now, he mused. Gemma's parents were overseas, and she said she had no other relatives, so his father had offered to walk her down the aisle. She'd thanked him and shocked them all by refusing. And she hadn't budged.

It didn't make a difference to the outcome. They were still going to be married today. Only his immediate family knew they weren't in love. The other guests had to be convinced they *were*. Tate didn't want his son growing up tainted by rumors that his father hadn't wanted him. As far as Nathan was concerned, he would know he was the reason for bringing his parents together. Today was really all about his son. And if Gemma let Tate down, then she'd be letting Nathan down, too. She knew a lot was riding on her performance today, hence her stunning entrance.

Just then, she reached the bottom of the stairs, took a moment to brace herself in an enchanting fashion and started her walk down the aisle.

His heart thumped as she came toward him, her eyes on his, not missing a step. She was most of the way, when her gaze slid sideways to the front row. An extremely cute Nathan in a little tuxedo was being cuddled in his grandmother's arms.

Without warning, Gemma stepped away to kiss her son on the cheek, causing a murmur of approval. Cameras clicked, and just that quickly he wondered if the loving gesture had been just to win the hearts of their audience. If so, it had done the trick.

She stepped back onto the red carpet and continued toward him. Up close, their eyes connected. He could see the nervousness on her face. All at once he found himself holding out his hand. After the briefest of hesitations, she accepted and slipped her palm in his. He brought her to him, lifted her hand to his lips and kissed it. She wasn't the only one who could make loving gestures, he told himself.

The ceremony began and Tate concentrated on that, not letting himself think about more than putting on a show. The vows seemed to be said by someone else, the wedding rings exchanged by another couple. He wouldn't let himself become sentimental. This was how it would be with any other woman.

Soon it was time to kiss the bride, and that's when Tate felt something inside him stumble. He'd *missed* kissing her.

He managed to look deep into her eyes, fully aware everyone would think the stare meant love. Only Gemma would see what he was truly saying.

Kiss like we mean it.

He dipped his head and placed his lips against hers. They were cool, and he could deal with that. He wanted cool between them. This show wasn't the place for passion. This was about sealing their vows with a kiss.

And then her lips quivered slightly, and without warning his mouth took on a life of its own. Her lips parted, her taste burst into his mouth.

A loud noise broke them apart, but it was reluctant on both sides. He caught the same sense of shock he felt reflected in Gemma's eyes before he turned to see that Nathan had dropped his toy car on the parquet floor.

"I think your little boy wants the attention now," the female celebrant said, and everyone laughed.

The ceremony was over.

"Yes, he's a natural," Tate agreed, glad to ignore how the softness of Gemma's lips had clung to his.

For show?

He didn't think so, he told himself, not happy about his part in that kiss either—nor the aftereffects of it. He'd thought he was immune to her. Now he knew he wasn't. How easily he could succumb to her charms again. He'd just have to make sure her lips weren't beneath his too often, if at all. Today was the exception.

"You'd better get used to the interruptions," an uncle said, approaching them with his wife at his side. Then the older man chuckled. "Look, Gemma's blushing already."

Tate saw pink tingeing her cheeks. "My blushing bride," he teased for the benefit of the others as he slipped her arm through his.

The official photographer took a couple of pictures, then others came up to wish them well, and somehow he and Gemma were separated. Frankly, he was surprised so many guests could come at such short notice. On the other hand, everyone liked good gossip, he thought with a touch of cynicism as he glanced through the French doors leading out to the terrace.

The extensive lawn had a large tent set up with tables and chairs as well as a dance floor. The landscaped gardens flowed down to a man-made lake. They'd decided not to have a formal wedding feast, merely the ceremony and as few speeches as possible, but plenty of food and drink and dancing if anyone was inclined.

His mother caught up with him, now minus her grandson. "Where's Nathan?" he asked.

"Bree's showing him off."

He smiled as he caught sight of his younger sister getting Nathan to clap hands for a few of the guests.

"That was a really lovely ceremony, darling."

He dragged his focus back to his mother, and the trace of hardness he always felt for her returned. "Yes, it was very convincing."

Her eyes flickered, noting the change in him, but she ignored it. "I do so wish Gemma's parents could have been here. It would have been nice if her father had walked her down the aisle."

"She was adamant about not interrupting their Mediterranean cruise."

"Hmm," his mother said, a frown creasing her forehead. "Something's not quite right there."

He agreed with his mother's assumption, but he had too much on his mind to worry about something that didn't concern him. "That's what Gemma wanted, so we respected that. It's none of our business."

Darlene sighed. "What a pity Drake couldn't make it either."

Tate stiffened. "Yes," he lied.

He hadn't called his best friend until a few days ago. He'd intended to point out it was best the other man didn't come to the wedding, but before he could say the words, Drake had wished him well and told him he couldn't get away. Tate knew that was just Drake's way of being a good friend, but it had been a relief.

"He's in Japan, you said," his mother continued as Gemma joined them.

"Drake's in the middle of trade negotiations." He felt Gemma freeze.

Tate wanted the subject changed.

Now.

"Still, he's your best friend. He should have been here."

Tate forced a smile for his new bride as he again slipped her arm through his. He wished his mother would shut the hell up. "Everything looks great, don't you think, Gemma?"

For a moment it didn't seem that she would manage a smile, but one appeared, if a little weak. "Yes, you've done a wonderful job, Darlene."

Darlene sent a really warm smile to her new daughter-in-law. "Thank you. I wanted it to be a special day for you both."

Then it was a pity she had mentioned Drake, Tate thought, surprised that his mother and Gemma had hit it off so well. Of course, the two women didn't know it, but they had a lot in common. Both of them had betrayed the men in their lives. Perhaps that's why his mother had a soft spot for Gemma.

And perhaps Gemma sensed it.

It would explain a lot.

Tate was grateful Bree chose that moment to come up to them carrying Nathan. He didn't want to think about what had happened between Gemma and Drake. She was *his* wife now. There would be no opportunity for those two to get together in the future. He'd make damn sure of it.

Gemma went to lift Nathan out of Bree's arms. "Here, let me hold him." She tried to pretend she hadn't heard Darlene and Tate talking about Drake. At least she now knew why the other man hadn't attended. Thank God he hadn't! She hadn't wanted to see him on her wedding day, but she hadn't dared mention him, or Tate might think she was interested.

She wasn't.

Not at all.

Her sister-in-law stepped back with a cool smile. "No, Nathan's fine. Besides, we don't want you to dirty that beautiful dress."

Gemma really didn't care about a dress that was off the rack, in spite of the fact that she and Nathan could have easily lived a year on the same amount of money. "That's okay, Bree."

"No, I insist. Besides, you and Tate need to circulate." It was a reminder of why this wedding was taking place.

"I'm happy to look after my nephew." Bree walked off with Nathan in her arms.

Under different circumstances, Gemma would have gone after her and taken back her son, but Nathan was chuckling as Bree bounced him on her hip, so Gemma let him be.

Anyway, Bree's issues were with Gemma, not Nathan. When she had commented on it, Tate had said his family knew nothing about their previous relationship. He'd said she must be imagining it. But Gemma was aware they all blamed her for keeping Nathan from them—everyone except Tate's mother, who was the only Chandler to show her some sympathy.

And Darlene had paid the price for it. Gemma had noticed some tension in the air. Even Tate showed a hint of reserve with his mother, though it wasn't something Gemma could put her finger on.

Just then two older ladies came up to them. "Oh, it was a lovely ceremony."

Gemma acknowledged that the Chandlers had pulled out all the stops to get the wedding arranged in such a short time. Needless to say, it was amazing what one could achieve when there was money to spare and family honor at stake.

"And so adorable how you gave your little boy a kiss on the cheek," the other woman said. "That was so sweet."

"Yes, that was inspired," Tate drawled, his meaning obvious, at least to her, though she noted Darlene gave him a sharp look.

Gemma ignored him. "Thank you. I wanted Nathan to be a part of it all."

"Well, you did that very well, my dear."

"It's good that he has both his parents now, don't you think?" the other lady said without menace.

Before Gemma could speak, Darlene stepped in, shepherding them away. "There's someone over there I want you both to meet."

"I didn't kiss Nathan for show," Gemma hissed at Tate, "despite what you obviously think."

"Really? You went above and beyond the call of duty with that one."

"It wasn't a duty."

"So you say."

"Drop dead, Tate," she said, the words falling out of her mouth before she could stop them.

He actually looked amused. "You'd like that, wouldn't you?"

"Married and widowed to you on the same day? Sounds good to me."

"You won't be so smart when we're alone later."

Her heart stuttered. "Wh-what?"

He stilled, then looked away. "Nothing," he muttered. "Not a thing."

She had the feeling that, like her, he'd spoken without thought. It had been the kind of thing they'd used to say when they were lovers. They hadn't discussed it, but she knew Tate would not let himself want her again. Their wedding kiss might have felt like a reunion for a few heartbeats, but neither of them would be caught out again.

More guests came up to them, and Gemma tried to act relaxed, but she was glad when Tate excused himself to speak to his grandmother and his father, who were holding court across the room. Bree approached them, and Tate lovingly scooped Nathan out of his sister's arms, making Gemma's heart lilt. She'd been watching Tate with Nathan these past ten days, and she had no doubt he loved his son. Nathan had grown used to Tate, too. They looked relaxed and comfortable together, these four generations of Chandlers.

She was the outsider.

And she'd probably never be a true part of this family. Add that to her own parents cutting her off and she suddenly felt like everyone in the world had deserted her.

Everyone but her son, she reminded herself.

Nathan loved her.

Nathan needed her like no one else.

How she wished it could be different with her own family. For her son's sake, she'd even phoned her parents to invite them to the wedding, hoping they might be pleased. After getting no answer, she'd phoned her father's work to learn they had gone on a Mediterranean cruise. She had to admit now that she was glad they weren't able to come. Her life was one big pretense, and she wasn't sure she could keep up the facade of happiness with them here. They'd hurt her too much.

At least Tate would be a far better parent to Nathan than her own parents had been to her, she thought, pushing aside her momentary self-pity as Nathan started to cry. Her poor little darling was overwhelmed and overtired. The doctor had said there were no complications from the operation, but Nathan could still be feeling the aftereffects.

She excused herself and went to him. "Ssh, Mommy's here, sweetie." She lifted Nathan out of Tate's arms, looking at the others. "It's his nap time. I'll take him upstairs." She was about to turn away when Tate's driver appeared at their side.

"Mr. Chandler, the reporters are here. They want to know when you and Gem—I mean, Mrs. Tate—will come out to see them."

Gemma groaned inwardly. She knew this was part of the deal, but not right now.

"Tell them they'll be there shortly, Clive," Jonathan Chandler said before Tate could speak. Then her father-in-law went to take Nathan from her. "We'll get one of the staff to take this boy upstairs while you and Tate do what you have to do."

Gemma instantly moved her son out of reach. "I'm sorry, Jonathan, but I intend to put Nathan to bed myself." She couldn't call him Mr. Chandler. She wouldn't. She doubted he'd ask her to call him "Dad."

"But the reporters—"

"Can wait," Gemma said quietly but firmly. Nathan needed her more than anyone else. And Lord knows, she needed the break.

"Gemma's right, Dad," Tate said, surprising her. "Nathan's needs are more important. The reporters can wait. They won't go away anytime soon." He gave a slight smile. "Unfortunately."

Jonathan looked from Tate to her and back again, then gave a sharp nod. "Okay, son."

Gemma had to bite her tongue. When *she* took a stand, she was ignored. When Tate took a stand, they listened. She hoped it wasn't going to stay this way her whole life.

Tate squared his shoulders. "I'll go talk to them, while Gemma goes upstairs." His gaze shifted to her. "Come down when you're ready."

Gemma was grateful to escape, but she wasn't sure she'd ever be ready to face them all. If only the day could be over.

Upstairs she gave Nathan a bottle and then changed his diaper in the small bedroom connected to hers.

"There we go, sweetie," she said, putting him in the crib. His eyes were closing as soon as his little head hit the pillow, and she smiled to see him sucking furiously on the bottle. For a few minutes she watched over him with all the love in her heart.

It wasn't until she went to leave the room that she realized she had a dilemma. Tate had bought the latest in digital baby monitors so she could hear Nathan no matter what room she was in, but she wasn't about to leave her son alone in here when a bunch of strangers were crawling all over the house.

Absolutely no way.

She looked out in the corridor, hoping to see someone who could pass a message to Tate, but there was no one. She even used the intercom for the kitchen, but no one answered. They were probably all too busy, maybe not even able to hear it. There was nothing to do but sit and wait it out. Tate would eventually come looking for her, she was sure. He had to. He needed her for the photographs.

About fifteen minutes later, someone knocked on her door and she hurried to open it. Tate stood there, his eyes showing his anger. "Is this some sort of protest?"

She angled her chin at his tone. "I guess it is."

"Not now, Gemma. We've got—"

"I'm not leaving Nathan up here alone."

He stopped and digested the info, then nodded. "I'll get Sandy to come up and stay with him."

Gemma had met Peggy and Clive's twenty-one-year-old daughter, and she was happy to leave Nathan with her. "No one's answering the intercom in the kitchen."

"I'll go get her." Ten minutes later he was back and was soon escorting Gemma down the staircase, her arm tucked under his as if it was the most natural thing in the world. "You made quite an entrance earlier."

She wouldn't let him know she'd been scared to death. "It's what you expected, wasn't it?"

"Yes, it's definitely something I would expect from you."

She hated the way he said that. "Actually, your mother suggested it."

"Did she now?" He remained quiet, but she wasn't sure what he thought about what she'd said.

Gemma was suddenly aware of Clive standing at the large front door, all set to open it to the reporters. When they reached the bottom step, she stopped. "Er…it's only going to be a couple of pictures, right?"

Tate looked at her oddly, then squeezed her arm. "A couple of photographs by the fountain, that's all. I'll answer the questions, but if they ask you anything, just do your best."

"Okay." Would her best be good enough?

He pulled her closer to his side. "Ready?"

She was surprised by his gesture, warmed that he wasn't quite prepared to feed her to the wolves. She cleared her throat. "Yes, as ready as I'll ever be."

Gemma wasn't sure how they pulled it off, but she and Tate managed to look like a loving couple as they stood in front of a spectacular fountain on the front lawn while a group of people took photographs. Hopefully any nervousness on her part was understandable.

And then…

"A kiss for the camera," one man suggested.

Almost imperceptibly, Tate's arm tensed beneath hers. For a moment she thought he would refuse. If only he would. She didn't want to relive the sensation of their last kiss.

Then his head rushed toward her, and he didn't miss another beat as he swept her into his arms like some romantic hero in a movie.

Lights.

Camera.

Action.

Even knowing this was all for show, her breath caught high in her throat. She fought not to let him take anything from her this time, but the kiss went on…and on…and on… Then, just as she started to yield, he released her.

His eyes gave nothing away, but she could see a slight flush to his cheeks. That, at least, made her feel less exposed.

With the practiced ease of someone who'd grown up in the spotlight, he turned to look at the photographers, a confident smile coating his lips. "Is that good enough, people?"

"Terrific!"

"Great!"

"Hey, what does the new Mrs. Chandler have to say about it?" a woman asked.

Gemma struggled to pick up her scattered senses. She had to play the game. If she showed how scared she was of the limelight, they'd chew her up and spit her out.

She gave what she thought was a convincing smile. "Practice definitely makes perfect."

Laughter erupted as the cameras clicked.

"Great quote! Now about—"

Tate put up his hand. "No more. My wife and I have a wedding to get back to." His mouth curved and he winked. "And a honeymoon." He started to lead her back inside.

"But what about the humanitarian award? What do you think about that?"

Tate stopped briefly. "I'm very proud of my family. It's an honor to receive such an award."

"And what about—"

Gemma saw a helicopter coming toward them in the distance.

Tate must have seen it, too, because he moved her toward the front door. "That's all, guys." They stepped inside and Clive closed the door behind them just as the chopper reached the estate.

"You'd better get on that, Clive, or they'll all be swarming overhead soon. They've got enough pictures now."

"Sure thing, Mr. Chandler." The other man hurried off.

Gemma's legs were shaky. "Thank God that's over," she managed to say.

As well as everything had gone, there was nothing quite as daunting as a helicopter overhead and a flock of reporters intent on finding a story. Any story.

Unless it was a comment from her new husband about a honeymoon...

He didn't mean it, she knew that. But still, it had shaken her, reminding her that Tate was a virile man and wouldn't remain celibate for long.

Would he take a lover?

The thought made her feel ill until she hurriedly decided he wouldn't. At least not yet. He wouldn't risk raining more bad press upon his family.

But would he want *her* eventually?

She believed that any sex between them would be full of hostility. Yet his kisses today hadn't been angry. She swallowed hard. That's because they'd had an audience, she told herself. It had all been for show. Nothing more.

Still, she'd started contraceptives last week as a precaution. The doctor had said they would take a month to work and had recommended using other precautions until then. She didn't expect to need them.

"It's not quite over yet," Tate said, bringing her focus back to the present. "We still have to return to our guests."

She forced aside her thoughts. She could handle the rest of the wedding. After that lot out there, it would be a piece of cake!

Perhaps she would rethink that, Gemma mused to herself, when a short time later she ended up alone with Tate's grandmother.

"I hope you'll treat my grandson right," Helen Chandler said, with that same coolness her granddaughter, Bree, showed to Gemma.

For a moment, Gemma thought Helen was talking about Nathan, then realized she meant Tate. "As long as Tate treats me and Nathan right, I will."

Helen inclined her head. "He will. My grandson knows his responsibilities."

"I'm sure." His sense of duty was the reason they were here today, wasn't it?

And then…Helen seemed to hesitate. "Tate takes things to heart. He feels deeply…like his father."

Gemma had the feeling that the older woman was trying to tell her something. After all, there was no question that Tate felt deeply. He thought he'd been deceived. First about Drake and then about his son, and both assumptions had greatly upset him. But was Helen talking about more than that? Was there something Helen knew that *she* didn't? Gemma couldn't think what.

Tate appeared in front of them. "I'm afraid I have to take Gemma away from you, Gran. We're expected to dance."

Expected? There was that responsibility thing again. Gemma suddenly felt like someone's cross to bear.

His cross.

She slipped smoothly into his arms, wishing she could

slip as easily into his life—or *out* of it—but neither was to be. "I know where you and your sister get it from now," she said, tilting her head up at him.

"What?"

"That attitude of yours. They're never going to forgive me, are they?"

"Gran's old."

"And Bree?"

"She's young, but her experience is light years away from yours."

Gemma swallowed her gall. He made it sound as if she'd been sleeping with the local football team. "As long as they don't take it out on Nathan, they can be as cool as they like to me."

"No one in my family will hurt my son."

"*Our* son."

He ignored her comment as they continued dancing, but their conversation got her thinking. The paternity test had been taken, but Tate hadn't mentioned it since. Maybe it took a while for the results to come in. Not that she was worried. Nathan could *only* belong to Tate.

"Your parents will be sorry they missed all this," Tate said, jolting her. She reacted without thinking.

"I'm sure."

He immediately scowled. "Why do you say—"

"Ouch!" she said, needing to change the subject.

"What's the matter?"

"My toe. You stepped on it," she fibbed.

She didn't want to discuss her parents. If they were here, it would only be out of duty, and she'd probably get upset. Why give Tate the chance to be more critical of her?

"I did? Sorry." He actually smiled. "I haven't done that since I was a teenager."

"Perhaps you're going through puberty again," she joked.

He chuckled, and, for a brief instant, they were on the same wavelength.

Like old times.

Only, it wasn't like old times, she reminded herself, quickly looking away.

Far from it.

The music ended and Tate led her over to his parents. Gemma was surprised to hear them talking about building a childproof fence around the gardens and grounds, to keep Nathan from accidentally wandering off or falling in the lake. For that, Gemma couldn't stop her heart from softening toward them, and she now regretted keeping Nathan from them for so long. As painful as it was to be married to a man who hated her, she was glad that Tate had accepted his son and glad Nathan had people around him who would always care for him. That was a huge comfort.

The afternoon came to a close after that, and the guests started to leave. Finally, only Tate's immediate family remained, and they said their goodbyes once the caterers had cleared up. It was an hour's drive back to the city, but everyone had agreed it wouldn't look good "honeymoon-wise" to have the in-laws staying in the house, no matter that it was the size of a football field.

The only people to stay were Peggy and Clive, and they were in separate quarters at the back of the house. Upstairs, she and Tate found Peggy's daughter on the floor playing with Nathan. It was a lovely picture, but as soon as Nathan saw them, he quickly crawled toward them.

Tate met him halfway and scooped him up. "Hey there, little man."

Gemma was happy to see father and son together, but

she couldn't help feeling a little weird. With the whirlwind of a wedding, she hadn't had the chance to think about Tate moving in on her territory. It had always been *she* who had scooped up Nathan. She who had received the first cuddle. Well, the only cuddle, really. There hadn't been any competition before.

Peggy's daughter left them to go back downstairs with her parents, and Tate's gaze flickered over Gemma's wedding gown. "I'll keep an eye on Nathan while you change."

She nodded and left the room. Last week he'd paid for the delivery of a wardrobe of expensive clothes. Thankfully, the sort of things she liked herself. Of course, what woman would say no to a new wardrobe? Especially when her clothes had been starting to wear thin.

Going into the other room, Gemma closed the door between them. Her hands shook as she changed into black slacks and a knit top, the quality of which couldn't be denied. They were so different from the blue jeans and T-shirts she'd always slipped into when she got home to her apartment.

Home was now with Tate.

Lord help her.

All at once she was aware of Tate's deep voice as he talked to his son in the other room. His voice alone used to make her knees wobble. Just as they were wobbling now.

His brief, detached glance didn't calm her nerves when she stepped back into the other room to find the two males playing on the floor.

Tate pushed to his feet and headed for the door. "I've got a couple of things to do. Call through to the kitchen when you're ready for dinner. Peggy will be happy to stay with Nathan if he's still awake."

Cold feet got the better of her. "Wait!" She swallowed

as he stopped. "Thank you, but I'd prefer to eat in my room tonight, if you don't mind."

His eyes turned frosty. "But I do mind."

"Tate, look." She tried to think. "Can't you let me have some time to myself? It's been a hectic day." It was an excuse, but it was a valid one.

"I'd be glad to leave you to it, but my mother arranged for Peggy to cook a special dinner in the small dining room, heaven knows why. So you're going to come down and we're going to eat it together. We start as we go on. Right?"

She could see he wasn't about to relent. She nodded. "Right."

"I'll see you downstairs at seven. If you want anything, call Peggy. She'll make sure you and Nathan have whatever you need." He twisted on his heels and left the room— and left her wondering how she would get through the evening.

At seven, Gemma went down to the smaller of the dining rooms, having changed into a dress for the occasion. Oh, she was going to be such a good little wife…in that respect anyway, she thought with a touch of cynicism. She'd follow instructions as necessary, and in public she'd be accommodating whenever it came to putting on a wifely show, but that was as far as it went. He'd coerced her into this marriage. She wasn't going to pretend to be happy about it.

Tate's eyes reflected fleeting approval, but all he said was, "He's asleep?"

"Yes." It had taken a while to get Nathan settled, but she had the baby monitor with her now and didn't have to worry about him waking up without her hearing. "He settled down. He just needed to have a cry."

"Don't we all," Tate mocked as he held out the seat for her.

Her heart lurched. The newness of her wedding ring suddenly weighed down her finger. She took a quick peek at his ring finger. Did he feel it as heavily?

The heated food warmers held an array of steamed vegetables and roasted meats, and a delicious-looking dessert. "It looks delicious," she said. Soft music played in the background, but it wasn't soothing.

"My mother thought we could do with something substantial after today." He sat down opposite her and poured some champagne. "Clive tells me there was barely any food in your apartment."

The words took her by surprise. She didn't want him to know how little food she had on hand. She'd lived on canned goods and bread. It was amazing what a person could do with a can of beans.

"He only mentioned it in passing yesterday," Tate added.

"He reports everything back to you, does he?" she said, already knowing the answer. "I didn't have time to shop, that's all."

Tate considered her. "You should eat more now. You could do with a little extra weight." He stared a moment more, then lifted his glass to her. "To us."

She could do with a drink of water rather than more alcohol. "You don't have to toast us, now that we're alone. It's not a proper wedding, Tate."

"Isn't it?"

She gave a soft gasp. "You don't mean—"

His face closed up as he put down his glass. "No, I don't mean that at all. I won't be sleeping with you tonight, Gemma. Not tonight, nor any night in the foreseeable future. I don't know if I can."

The ability to speak deserted her. He disliked everything about her and didn't intend to overcome it, not even to exercise the physical desire they'd once shared. Regardless of her fear that she'd be a pushover if they were to make love, a deep hurt rolled through her. It was one thing to know he had a grudge against her. It was quite another to realize the depth of his animosity.

She raised her chin with a cool stare. "I didn't ask you to sleep with me, Tate, but at least leave me with *some* dignity. I may not be the perfect wife, but you don't have to make me feel like I'm something that crawled out of the gutter."

He stiffened. "I'm sorry. I just don't want you thinking I might be tempted, that's all."

She managed a cynical smile. "Oh, believe me, I know you're not tempted. But I'm not interested either. So rest easy, Mr. Chandler. Your virtue is intact."

"I'm glad we've made that clear."

"Perfectly." Willing her hands not to shake, she reached to serve herself some of the vegetables and meat, even though her appetite had disappeared. Tate had said they'd start as they'd go on, and she would make sure she did. Today, tomorrow—it was all about Nathan. She would remind herself of that as often as she could.

They didn't talk much as they ate, except for a few things about the wedding. Tate mentioned giving Peggy the night off after such a long day, but Gemma didn't think for a minute he had any ulterior motives.

It seemed a long meal and one she didn't look forward to repeating night after night. It would only remind her of other dinners during their affair when conversation had been easy and led straight to sex.

Finally they'd finished dessert. She was just about to refuse coffee and make her escape when Tate drew a plain white envelope from his pocket and slid it along the tablecloth.

Her brows drew together as she picked it up. "What's this?"

"The results of the paternity test."

The envelope almost fell from her fingers. Then she saw it was sealed. She looked up. "You haven't read it?"

"No."

Could he be saying he was prepared to take her word that Nathan was his? Her heart thumped as she asked the question. "Why not?"

"I wanted to prove I would marry you without knowing the results and without taking your word for it. *That's* how sure I am Nathan is my son."

"I see." He hadn't married her because he believed her. He'd married her because he'd believed in *himself,* in his gut feeling that Nathan was his son. Nothing else. He was saying he didn't trust her—not even with a truth he himself believed. She'd known Tate felt this way. She'd accepted it. But she felt a fool for doubting it for just this instance.

"Aren't you going to open it, Gemma?"

She hesitated, not because she didn't know what it would say, but because she was still trying to pull herself together.

"It doesn't matter to me if you open it or not," he continued. "The results are still the same."

She had no doubt, but she had to read it—for Nathan's sake. She quickly opened it, scanned it, then passed the sheet of paper to Tate.

He didn't hesitate as he took it from her. Didn't hesitate as he read it and said easily, "He's mine."

It was a statement of fact.

"Yes."

He sat in the chair and nodded, almost to himself, looking

pleased but not surprised. Then he began tearing the paper in half, then quarters.

Her eyes widened. "What are you doing?"

"We don't need to keep any proof." He let the pieces sprinkle down on the tablecloth.

Her forehead creased. "But don't you want your family to know the truth?"

"They already know all they need to know. I've said he's my son, and they can see he is. I don't need to show them proof. My word is good enough."

It must be wonderful to have a family who believes in you, in what you say and do. She was quite envious of Tate for that.

And now Nathan would be part of such a family, she reminded herself. Now more than any other time today, she felt she'd done the right thing in marrying Tate. She may not love Tate madly like she'd once thought she did, but it took a special man to offer marriage for the sake of a child not proven to be his. Tate had even begun to love a son without proof that he was the father. For that alone, a small pocket of her heart would always belong to Tate Chandler.

Four

Gemma wasn't surprised that she woke early the next morning. Nathan had slept through the night, and she'd fallen asleep as soon as her head hit the pillow. She'd probably even snored, so it was just as well that Tate hadn't shared her bed.

Her heart cramped at the thought, as she looked up at a high ceiling as untouchable as her new husband.

She understood that he didn't want to share her bed, but it still hurt. It filled her with despair to know she had to live with a man who wouldn't let himself want her, now nor in the future. She had done nothing wrong!

It wasn't fair.

But did she really want someone who couldn't trust her? To be truthful, deep down she did still want Tate. She wasn't *in love* with him. It was all purely physical. But knowing that didn't change a thing.

Thank God physical attraction was something she could teach herself to ignore.

Starting right now.

She threw back the covers, glad to escape her thoughts, and sneaked a peek at Nathan, who was still sleeping. She showered and dressed, and by the time she was ready, Nathan was awake and hungry. She quickly clothed him, then took him downstairs in search of food.

In the kitchen, Tate was eating a bowl of cereal at the island. Her pulse raced, but she tried to ignore it. She'd seen him each morning for the past ten mornings, though his focus had been on Nathan or the wedding or business.

Today, his hooded eyes told her he had heard her coming.

"Good morning." His gaze moved to his son and lit up, filling with a warmth that had once been for her. "How is he this morning?"

"Hungry." She couldn't be jealous of her son, but Tate's reaction was another reminder that things had changed a great deal between them.

"He's a growing boy, aren't you, sport?" Tate smiled at his son with an indisputable look of fatherly love.

She wrenched her gaze away. This all could have been so different…*should* have been so different.

"Peggy not around this morning?" she managed to say as she carried Nathan into the pantry, where Peggy had put the baby food. More often than not, Gemma fed her son fresh food, but the jars came in handy sometimes.

"Clive was going to drive their daughter back to the city, so I told Peggy to go with him and take the day off." He raised his voice to reach her. "They'll return this evening. I assured her we could look after ourselves."

"I'm sure we can." Gemma was suddenly relieved he

couldn't see her face. This would be the first time she and Tate would be alone—except for Nathan—in the house together since they'd run into each other at the hospital. And they were supposed to be on their "honeymoon," making the situation seem intimate.

Tate looked up as she exited the pantry with the food. He put down his spoon. "Here, give Nathan to me while you heat that up."

"No, that's okay. You finish your breakfast. I'll put him in his high chair."

Tate pushed his bowl aside and came toward them. "I'd really like to hold my son, Gemma."

He met her gaze, boldly showing her his fatherly side. It gave her an odd feeling, sort of squishy inside. She handed Nathan over without a word and went to heat up some milk to go with the oatmeal. At least Tate didn't hold back on emotion where their son was concerned.

"Do you want to feed him?" she asked.

Tate looked up in surprise. "Sure." He cleared his throat. "Thanks."

It was silly to warm to him just because he wanted to feed his son, but she did anyway. "Okay, put him in the highchair first." She waited while he fastened the safety belt, then passed Tate the bowl and spoon. "Now just spoon it into his mouth. You've seen me do it. It's easy."

Tate scooped up the mushy food, then hesitated. Gemma had to smile. It was amazing that this successful businessman, with confidence seeping from every pore, actually looked nervous.

"He's waiting for his breakfast," she pointed out.

That pushed Tate into action. He moved the first spoonful toward Nathan, who instantly opened his mouth. Tate's eyebrows shot up. "Hey, this is easy."

Something lightened in the room.

She gave a soft laugh. "Of course it is."

"Clearly he's an amenable chap," he said, winking at her. "Must take after me."

Gemma wasn't sure who was more taken aback by that wink—her or Tate. She was certain it wasn't something he had done intentionally, especially when he averted his eyes again to scoop up another spoonful of food.

Still, it was nice to have a cheerful mood between them, if only for a few minutes. "Yes, well, he's hungry right now. You should try getting him to open his mouth when he's *not* hungry."

Tate slipped another spoonful in his son's mouth. "I can't believe that."

"You *did* say he took after you," she joked.

Tate's gaze returned to her, one eyebrow quirking, his eyes amused. "So you're calling my son and me stubborn?"

"*Obstinate* is the word I would have used."

"Oh, really," he drawled.

Their gazes linked...

It was like old times...

Suddenly they were talking on one level but aware of each other on another. She stood close enough to see the attraction flare in his eyes.

He was the first to break eye contact, turning back to his son. "What are your plans for this morning?" His voice was neutral, as if the camaraderie had never been.

Disappointment rippled through her, followed by anger at herself. Why be disappointed because their one moment of bonding was over? It couldn't make up for the rest of the issues between them.

The rest of their lives...

And his question made it sound as if he wasn't hoping to share the day with her either, which was a relief. She could be herself without him around. She didn't have to defend the person she was.

"I thought I might take Nathan for a walk around the gardens and down to the lake. It's a beautiful day."

He nodded. "Good idea. He needs fresh air and sunshine. He's a bit pale."

Was there an implied criticism in his words? Was he saying their son hadn't been getting proper care and attention because she'd been a single, working mother? If so, that just wasn't true. He was at a wonderful daycare while she worked, and every weekend she'd made sure Nathan got out and about with her. They went to the beach or a park, or even the local supermarket where she'd do her weekly shopping. He'd always had fun there, charming the cashiers with his smile. Gemma had loved showing him off.

"I know Nathan can't go swimming yet," Tate said, reminding her that the doctor had said it was best to wait awhile before putting Nathan in the water, and even then he would have to wear a special cap to cover his ears. "But the pool is there anytime for you to use. It's not quite summer, but it's heated and you won't get cold."

His consideration surprised her. "Thanks. It'll be nice to have some time to swim by myself." As soon as she said the words, she held her breath. Would Tate think she had an ulterior motive? Would he think she was suggesting *he* join her in the pool?

His eyes closed in on her, but not in the way she might expect. "Gemma, you realize we have to stay here for the full week or it won't look right?"

Everything inside her went thud. "I know you don't want to be with me, Tate. You don't have to keep telling me."

He cursed softly. "You're losing sight of something. This isn't about us. I'm doing this for my family's sake, and in the long run for Nathan." He allowed a tiny pause. "I thought you were, too."

How did he manage to turn everything to his advantage? She gave a sigh. "Yes, of course I am."

"Then what's the problem?"

There was an empty ache in the region of her heart, but she ignored it. "No problem. You're the one seeing problems where there's none."

He stared hard, clearly not liking her answer. Then he gave Nathan the last spoonful of food and pushed to his feet. "I'll be in the study all morning."

The chill was back.

And yet as he went to leave, he stopped to ruffle his son's hair in a brief but loving caress. Gemma saw the gesture and realized Tate was right. For a moment, she *had* lost sight of the reason for their marriage. This was about Nathan. She just had to get used to there being nothing for *her*.

Once in the study, Tate tried to concentrate on a thick business report but soon gave up and went to stand by the window. His mind was on Gemma, and he needed to follow his thoughts or they would drive him insane. Just like the woman herself.

As much as he hated to admit it, he wanted her. He wanted her in a big way. And that's what it came down to between them—the *only* thing between them.

Want.

A want like no other.

God, how did he continue to want a woman who'd used him like she had? And how could he exorcise her from his system now that she was a part of his life? By ignoring the wanting, that's how. By refuting it every time it reared its head, like he had last night over dinner, and again this morning in the kitchen. He couldn't forget seeing her kissing Drake two years ago. The memory was tattooed on his brain. Her physical attributes might temporarily block it out, but it always returned, full force. The future looked dark indeed.

It was all her fault, so why was he feeling rotten about it?

Women!

He loved his mother, but she had let his father down badly. And Gemma had let *him* down badly. He hadn't learned to trust his mother again. He wasn't sure he could learn to trust Gemma. Not for a long time, he decided, as he saw Gemma pushing Nathan's stroller along the path toward the lake.

The urge to join them was strong. And it had nothing to do with those long legs of Gemma's showcased by her slim slacks. Heaven help him if she decided to strip down to a swimsuit and use the pool. He knew every inch of her luscious body, remembered every taste of her delicious skin and the husky sounds she made beneath him, the heavenly feel of being inside her.

Remembering was suddenly too much.

He had to concentrate on other things. Things like Nathan. The child who *was* his son. The paternity test had only proven what he'd already known. He couldn't even explain how he'd known the connection between him and Nathan was there.

He'd just known.

Just like he knew that if they were spending the week here, the child would need to be occupied. And what *he* needed to do was concentrate on Nathan's needs and not his own.

Right.

Nathan couldn't swim yet because of his ears, so a

sandbox and some toy trucks sounded like just the ticket. A friend had bought their son one, and the boy had loved it.

After taking one more look to check that Gemma and Nathan were okay as they reached the lake, Tate went to his laptop and searched the internet for a local toy store. It was much more interesting than reading a report.

After Gemma had tidied up the kitchen, she'd changed Nathan into cute little jeans and a T-shirt. Next, sunscreen on them both, she got his stroller and headed out. Tate had insisted they bring the stroller, though she hadn't thought she would need it. But now his reason became obvious. He hadn't intended to spend more time with them—with her—than necessary, and had probably been trying to ease his conscience, figuring she at least wouldn't have to carry Nathan around everywhere.

How caring of her new husband, she'd mused cynically.

Now, as she pushed Nathan's stroller along a side path down to the lake, the sunshine melted her cynicism. It was so beautiful and peaceful out here, with a light spring breeze playing over the rolling countryside, making her feel as if she were walking in a private park.

The lake was even more breathtakingly gorgeous up close, partly surrounded by trees and with a gazebo close by. Along the water's edge, patches of tall reeds partially hid nests of swans, while others quietly glided on the water, creating gentle ripples over the reflective depths.

Gemma decided to take Nathan out of his stroller and carry him to the water's edge to show him the swans, when she heard a noise over in a group of trees. She twisted toward the sound, thinking it was Tate, her heart missing a beat. Only it wasn't Tate. A young teenager came out of the shadows, walking his horse toward the lake.

He jolted when he saw her. "Oh. Sorry. I didn't know anyone else was here."

She stared, not really sure what to say.

"I'm Rolly." He pulled a face. "Roland, actually. My dad works for the people over the rise there. I help him out. They let me exercise their horses."

He looked to be around eighteen and didn't appear threatening, so Gemma relaxed a little. "I'm Gemma, and this is my son, Nathan."

He nodded as his gaze slid to her son then back. "I'd heard there was a wedding here yesterday." He glanced toward the stroller near the gazebo steps. "Tate's not with you?"

She was immediately on her guard and realized that from here she couldn't be seen from the house. The young man didn't look dangerous, but who was to say this Rolly was who he said he was? He could be a reporter, and even if he wasn't, she wasn't about to say too much.

"He had to make a phone call, but he'll be here shortly."

All at once, he seemed to sense her nervousness. "In case you're wondering, I'm allowed to bring the horses here to drink. Mr. Chandler said I could."

"You mean Jonathan?" she said, thinking of Tate's father.

"No, Nathaniel." His expression clouded. "He was a nice old man. We used to play chess together sometimes when he was here."

From all accounts, that sounded like something Tate's grandfather would do. "I'm sure you'll be welcome to keep on doing that." It was the country way, after all.

He fell into a grin. "Thanks."

She smiled back, touched to see a genuine smile for a

change. The past two weeks had been all about putting on a brave face, or a cool face, when she felt nothing like that inside.

The horse wandered to the water's edge and began to drink. "That's a nice horse. He's a lovely color."

"He's a young racehorse."

"I don't know much about horses except that they like to eat hay."

Rolly chuckled. "Yeah, hay and other things. This guy has a particular sweet tooth. I give him an apple sometimes. Not often though." He patted the horse's side. "Do you ride?"

"No. I've been pretty busy." She didn't say she'd never ridden a horse in her life. As nice as he was being to her, she should keep her distance. "Well, I'd best go and see what's keeping Tate. It was nice meeting you, Rolly."

"You too, Gemma." He hesitated. "I come down here most days around this time. In case you want some company."

He seemed to understand more about her than she'd assumed. He was offering a hand of friendship. It was very generous of him, and she appreciated it.

She smiled. "I'll keep that in mind." She went over to the stroller to strap Nathan back in. It only took a few moments. "Stay as long as you like," she added as she straightened.

"Okay. Thanks again."

Gemma headed back to the house with a lighter step. It was silly, but she really did feel as if she had made a friend, someone who had no real connection to the Chandlers and their condemnation. It was a pleasant relief, and one she wouldn't spoil by mentioning it to Tate. He probably wouldn't be interested anyway.

All was quiet as she stepped inside the kitchen, and she

was surprised to see that an hour had passed. There was no sign of Tate, so she made herself a cup of coffee and gave Nathan a biscuit and a drink. They went into the sunroom, where he crawled around on the floor and played with a collection of small plastic containers she'd brought from the kitchen. The items kept him occupied for some time.

When he started to get tired, she carried him upstairs and put him to bed, taking the baby monitor with her downstairs. Now, alone, she finally had time to get her bearings. There were a variety of formal and informal living areas, a conservatory, a room with a pool table, another with a spa. Gemma wasn't surprised Tate hadn't mentioned the latter; they'd made full use of the spa in his penthouse two years ago.

Shying away from the memories, Gemma continued past the study door, now firmly closed, and headed back to the relaxed warmth of the sunroom, where she sat on a recliner and read a magazine. After a while, the warm room made her feel drowsy. Soon she closed the pages and leaned her head back, shutting her eyes for a mere moment...

The next thing she knew, a warm hand on her shoulder shook her awake. Her eyelids flew open and air escaped her lungs as she looked straight into Tate's blue eyes. His intense look made her wonder how long he'd been watching her. In that one split second, what they'd had between them came rushing back—the excitement, the adrenaline rush, the sweet torment of bringing each other to climax...

Her stomach gave a quiver as she hastily sat up. Thankfully he moved back, and the moment was lost.

Forever? She'd thought so, but now she wasn't sure.

"It's past twelve," he said, his voice sounding slightly gruff.

She pushed to her feet and tidied her hair. "You want lunch, I suppose."

He scowled. "Yes, but I'm not asking you to do it. You're my wife now, Gemma, not my servant."

She liked that he wasn't taking advantage of their relationship, and an odd tenderness wove through her even as she chastised herself for being such a pushover. Good Lord. What was she thinking by offering to make him lunch? He had a perfectly good pair of hands.

Dream hands, in fact.

The golden touch.

Oh, yeah, how often she had succumbed to his touch.

She cleared her throat. "I'd better go check on Nathan. He should be awake soon." Taking the baby monitor with her, she left the room.

When she went back downstairs with Nathan, Tate had laid out their lunch on the island in the center of the kitchen. Nathan's high chair was already seated next to it.

"Why don't you feed him, then we'll eat," Tate suggested, and she nodded, liking that he wanted his son's needs met first.

Once that was done, Nathan was happy to play with a spoon while she and Tate ate their lunch of cold cuts and salad. Then Tate surprised her by saying, "By the way, I've got a delivery coming this afternoon."

She lifted a brow. "A delivery?"

"For Nathan. He needs some toys."

She frowned. "But he's already got toys."

"He doesn't have an outside play area, so I've ordered one of those shell-shaped sandboxes, plus a bucket and spade, a toy wagon, a toy lawn mower and some other things he'll enjoy."

"Other things?" Just how much had he ordered?

"A plastic pit with balls and an activity center that will keep him busy. Those are for inside. There are a couple of other things, too." He gave a slight shake of his head. "It's amazing the toys available these days. Very educational, too. I've ordered two sets of everything. One for here and one for when we get back to the city."

"Did you order the whole store?" she joked.

The corners of his mouth quirked upward. "Are you making fun of me?"

His affability was disconcerting, but she hid the feeling behind a small smile. "Never."

His mouth twisted wryly. "You think it's overkill, don't you?"

"Well…yes. I think a little. He's not even walking yet."

"He will be soon though." Tate's brows drew together. "Won't he?"

She nodded, endeared by his hesitation despite herself. "I'm told they usually start to walk about now, but every child is different. It could be a few more months," she warned, so he didn't get his expectations too high.

Tate took that in, then nodded. "He'll be fine. As you say, he'll do it in his own time." For a moment his eyes rested on his son with pride. When he turned back to Gemma, he was all business again. "They probably won't get here until around five. Unfortunately, I couldn't get it any earlier."

"When did you place the order?"

"Not long ago."

And he expected it to be here in a few hours? It always amazed her how fast he could buy things. The world of the uber-rich was certainly different. Her own upbringing in a middle-class family didn't come close to the privilege and entitlement afforded to a family like the Chandlers.

"I'll see Dad about getting the pool fenced off, too," Tate said, drawing her from her thoughts.

She tilted her head. "Will your parents mind about the play area?"

"Not at all. They've probably already thought of it. And they've said they wanted to put a childproof fence around the lake, remember? Anyway, it won't be an issue until he's walking."

She loved that he was so protective of Nathan's well-being.

After lunch, Tate went to clear the table, but she waved him aside. She needed something to do while he went back to his study. She wasn't used to having time on her hands. She'd always been working, and even these past ten days had been full with rushing to get ready for the wedding. Now, she looked down the long stretch of the afternoon with only a toy delivery on the agenda.

Enough! she told herself as she cleaned up the kitchen while chatting to Nathan in his high chair. Spending time with her son was exactly what she'd been longing to do. Now she could do that. She wouldn't waste a moment of it.

Once in the right frame of mind, the afternoon flew by, then just before five, the delivery van arrived. Tate told the man to drive around back, and Gemma let Nathan play on the floor of the sunroom as she watched Tate help unload a large plastic sandbox.

The rest of the items were soon dispensed with, and she watched a few minutes more as Tate asked questions about the other bits and pieces. She couldn't help noticing that for someone born with a silver spoon in his mouth, Tate got on well with people of all levels, even as he kept a slight reserve that was inherent in his personality.

By the time she heard the van depart, Gemma was

sitting on a stool in the kitchen feeding Nathan his dinner. A couple of minutes later, Tate appeared in the doorway.

"Oh." He looked disappointed. "He's eating."

"Sorry, he usually eats around now, and I didn't want to wait any longer." She used to collect Nathan from the day-care center around four-thirty each afternoon, and he was more than ready for his dinner by the time they got home and she had prepared it. Then she used to have an hour of play and bath time with her son. It was wonderful to be able to do it all now without rushing.

Tate nodded. "Yes, you're right." Then he looked down at himself and grimaced at the black streaks on his trousers and marks on his shirt. "I need a shower."

At the mention of water sluicing down his body, she felt her cheeks heat up. She looked away and continued feeding Nathan as she tried to push aside her memories of sharing a shower with Tate. "Um…we can have dinner around seven." A few seconds lapsed, and she glanced up. He was giving her hot cheeks an intense look. "I'll be bathing Nathan after this," she added, trying to cover the awkward moment.

His expression changed. "I'd like to give him his bath, if that's okay with you."

She blinked in surprise. "*You* want to bathe Nathan?"

"Sure." His jaw tightened. "I know I haven't been around as much as I'd have liked these past ten days, but that's going to change."

Why? she wanted to ask, both of them knowing he could have spent more time with his son today, both of them knowing why he hadn't. This was about avoiding spending too much time with *her*. Regret washed over her that Nathan had to unknowingly suffer because she and Tate had personal issues.

"Anyway," Tate's voice drew her back to him, "I got

some last-minute things out of the way, so tomorrow Nathan and I will be able to spend more time together."

Time with his son.

Not with his wife.

"I'm sure he'd like that," she said, keeping her voice neutral.

There was a moment's pause, as if Tate were trying to read more into her answer, but she kept her eyes averted, not letting him see anything on her face. They both knew the score.

"Maybe we'll go for a drive in the afternoon," he said.

Her gaze snapped instantly to him. "You mean you and Nathan?"

He frowned. "You as well."

"Oh." She hadn't expected that. A feeling of joy raced through her, even though she knew she shouldn't get her hopes up.

A shadow crossed his face, then he pivoted away. "I'll go take that shower now," he muttered, and strode through the kitchen to the back stairs.

Gemma waited for him to disappear before she let the tension leave her body. She'd thought her question reasonable under the circumstances, yet it had seemed to surprise him. Needless to say, she couldn't automatically assume she would be included in all the activities he shared with their son. Hadn't she been preparing herself for that reality ever since he'd seen Nathan at the hospital?

But as she continued to feed Nathan, she realized there was something more significant going on here. Tate had willingly suggested they do something together that wasn't for show. It was almost as if he'd offered to go for a drive with her, whether Nathan was with them or not. It was almost as if he wouldn't mind spending time in her company. Could that mean he was beginning to trust her?

And why did that suddenly make her feel so good?

Tate stood under the shower, hoping the water would loosen the knot in his gut. Did Gemma really think he would leave her at home tomorrow and take off with Nathan by himself? How could she think she wasn't invited? She was the mother of his son, for heaven's sake. He wouldn't leave her behind. It wouldn't look right. She was his wife now, and they had to act their parts.

The truth was that it wouldn't *be* right to leave her at home. Just what sort of person did she think he was? He winced. Okay, so he knew, but despite remembering their breakup, he only had to look into her blue eyes to feel like a heel.

He could handle her anger. He could even handle her hurt. She had brought all this on herself. But sometimes he saw more in those enticing depths.

The memory of what he'd once felt for her shook him up. Why this particular woman got to him, he didn't know. He wished to hell he could ignore his desire for her, but he couldn't. In the meantime there was only one thing for it.

Tate blasted his heated blood with cold water until it turned to ice.

By the time he dressed, he was ready for anything— until he went into the other suite, drawn by the sound of running water. He stopped dead in the doorway, watching as Gemma leaned forward and squirted bubble bath while swirling the water with her other hand. She'd kicked off her shoes.

The vision of her very nice rear view made him want to walk lazy fingers over her. Lord, he remembered how well the cheeks of her bottom fit his hands as he'd pulled her naked body against him. Those cheeks were a little more lusciously rounded than before, but she'd had a baby since he'd last known her, touched her...

He coughed, more for himself than to alert her to his presence. Otherwise he could easily stand here all evening appreciating that view.

She looked over her shoulder. "You're back." She put the bottle of bubble bath on the sink, then straightened, a flush on her cheeks.

"And ready for bath time," he said as a joke, only it came out husky.

Her gaze slid down his chest, then back up again.

Their eyes met.

She pushed past him, heading to the playpen. "I'll get Nathan ready."

It wouldn't have taken much to pull her to him. Nor would it have taken much to put her against the door and kiss every inch of that creamy skin. Only, he didn't. He followed her, watching her dart a nervous look over her shoulder as she picked Nathan up. For a couple of seconds, the sexual stimulation of pursuing Gemma called to something inside him.

With effort he put the feeling aside. "He likes a bath, does he?"

Relief that was no doubt due to the change of subject crossed her face as she began undressing the baby. "He loves it. He cries whenever I take him out."

She looked away and placed a special cap on Nathan to protect his ears before swinging him toward Tate, a determined angle to her chin. "Here we go. One little boy." She went back into the bathroom. "I'll just check the water's still the right temperature."

Tate followed her, his eyes drawn once more to her slim figure leaning over the tub.

"Just right," she said, straightening.

Hell, yeah.

"Your clothes might get wet."

"No problem."

A frisson of awareness entered her eyes. It was for the best that Nathan squirmed and insisted on his full attention right then. He eased his son into the warm, sudsy water and got down on his knees on the fluffy bathmat, fully aware of Gemma moving out of touching distance.

But his son wouldn't be ignored. Tate was soon engrossed in games with Nathan. "This really is fun," he mused, half to himself.

"You sound surprised."

He looked up. "I didn't know it could be like this," he admitted, startled to feel his chest squeeze tight with emotion. He quickly looked back down at the water, not wanting her to see just how much this was affecting him.

"It's awesome, isn't it?" she said softly, as if she knew exactly what he was feeling.

"Yeah." He cleared his throat, but he didn't look up. "Awesome."

More playtime followed, and as much as he was enjoying it, he was beginning to realize how tiring an infant could be. It must have been hard for Gemma to juggle a job as well as look after a baby all by herself. In spite of his animosity toward her, he had to admit to a growing admiration for her.

"That water will be getting cool now," she said eventually, unfolding a towel.

Tate felt the coolness of the water and nodded. Then he reached for the plug.

"Don't!"

His hand stopped. "What's the matter?"

"The sound of the water going down the hole frightens him."

He couldn't hold back a small laugh. "That's cute."

"You wouldn't say that if you heard him screaming his lungs out," she teased, holding up the towel.

Tate picked up Nathan from the bath, and she engulfed the child in the fluffy material and then handed him back. "You can finish off the job, while I tidy up in here."

"I'm not sure who's getting the better deal here," he drawled, trying not to show his lack of confidence in his parenting abilities. Her eyes said she was enjoying this.

"You have to learn to dress him sometime."

He looked down at his son then back up at her. "I'll pay you a thousand dollars to do it for me."

She gave a tinkling laugh, and the sound did crazy things to his pulse. "Not on your life."

His eyes locked on her mouth...

And her smile froze...

She twisted toward the bath. "I'd better clean up in here."

He paused before moving toward the bedroom. "I'll shut the door so he won't hear you emptying the bath."

"Thanks."

He closed the door behind him on the way out, took a breath to let his pulse settle, then looked down at his son. "Okay, sport. Let's get you sorted."

And no more thinking about that smile of Gemma's, he told himself, as he carried Nathan to the changing table. He gave the baby a squeaky toy, continuing to talk to him in case he could hear the bath water going down the drain.

He was still standing at the changing table when he saw

the bathroom door open. He looked up at Gemma with relief and conceded defeat. "I need your help."

She came toward them. "With what?"

"Please show me how to put on a diaper. I can't seem to get it right."

Her lips twitched with the amusement of an all-knowing mother. "For a start, that's the wrong way."

"It is?"

"And you've worn the adhesive off the tabs."

"I was trying to get it right."

She ruefully shook her head. "Move aside." In one quick motion, she'd grabbed another diaper from the pack, did a few things with it, lifted Nathan's bottom, removed the old and put the new one under him. "See. This is how—"

Tate was concentrating when something arced in the air and splashed across his chest. "What the—"

Gemma blinked, then giggled.

He looked down at his shirt. It had been damp a moment ago but was now wet. She giggled even louder as she pulled up the front flap of the diaper and covered their son's private parts.

All at once Tate saw the humor, too. "I guess that's what happens when you have a boy."

She held the diaper in place with one hand as her giggle turned to laughter. "Oh, my God…" more laughter, "you should see…" laugh, "the look on your…face."

He had to chuckle. "Stop laughing, Gemma."

"I ca-can't."

His laughter increased, and all at once they were both laughing together. Really laughing. It seemed so long since they'd shared something this funny.

Then, "I've always thought you had a lovely laugh," he murmured, unable to stop himself.

Her amusement stilled, and she moistened her top lip with her tongue. "You did?"

His gaze dropped to the tip of that pink tongue. "I've told you that before, surely?"

Her eyes flickered. "No, I would have remembered."

Suddenly there was something more between them than their love for their son. "Would you?"

"Yes."

Several heartbeats ticked by. He knew his head was lowering toward her. He couldn't stop himself.

Then Nathan squeaked his toy and they both jumped. Gemma hastily turned back to their son, who she was still holding on the changing table with one hand. Tate blew out an unsteady breath.

They'd been getting too intimate. He stepped back. "I'll go change my shirt."

She flicked him a look. "I'll put Nathan to bed, then I'll check on the dinner."

"Fine." By that time he fully intended to be detached again.

Yet, as he went back to his room, he tried to analyze what was happening between him and Gemma. He didn't want to like her, but she kept slipping under his guard. His only excuse was that sharing a bond over their son was getting to him, causing the awareness between him and Gemma to build.

Neither of them wanted this...

Both of them wanted this...

Five

Gemma dreamed that Tate was saying she had a lovely laugh, and—oh, God—he was about to kiss her…willingly…

Then she opened her eyes and deep disappointment ripped through her. He wasn't about to kiss her at all. It was morning. She was in bed. And Tate wasn't with her.

And it was *his* fault she'd been dreaming about him all night. He *had* been about to kiss her last night after they'd bathed Nathan. He *had* been tempted, in spite of his earlier assertions that he wasn't.

Of course, once they'd gone downstairs he'd made it quite clear he wouldn't let her get so close again. They'd eaten their casserole then he'd gone to the study while she'd watched a movie. Alone. The home movie theater wasn't the largest of rooms, but it had felt empty. She wondered if he would keep to his promise of taking them for a drive today.

Right then, she heard Nathan's chuckle from next door. She threw back the blankets and hopped out of bed, slipping on her robe as she hurried to the connecting door. She found Tate on the floor playing peek-a-boo with Nathan, who was in his playpen. Her son looked incredibly adorable standing up, holding on to the rails in his pajamas.

And Tate looked so relaxed and carefree.

The old Tate.

Then he looked at her and the wary new Tate slipped back into place. "Did we wake you?"

"Yes, but it was time for me to get out of bed anyway." She wanted to step into the room to give her son a morning kiss but was conscious of the word *bed* and Tate's gaze on her silky robe. She remained where she stood.

"You were sleeping very peacefully," he said, his eyes lifting back to her face.

So he'd checked on her. The image unnerved her. "I was tired."

He scowled. "Are you okay?"

His concern took her by surprise, and warmed her. "Better for a good night's sleep." And that was something she wouldn't have had if he'd been sharing her bed.

As if he read her thoughts, the words suddenly transported them to last evening—and their almost-kiss right here in this room…right there beside the changing table.

Stop!

She grabbed for something to break the silence. "Er…I should change Nathan's diaper."

"Done."

She couldn't have made a joke about that if her life had depended on it. Breaking eye contact, she mentally scrambled to pull herself together. "If you could mind him a little longer, I'll shower then take him down for breakfast."

"That's okay, I'll take him downstairs with me." Tate got to his feet, all business now. "By the way, Peggy and Clive are back."

"They are?" The other couple must have left the city before dawn to get here.

He swung Nathan up in his arms. "We'll be in the sunroom. Take your time." He crossed to the other door and left her standing in the connecting doorway.

After he left, she took a ragged breath, then she hurried to the shower. It was better that Clive and Peggy had returned. Having others in the house could diffuse the growing tension between her and Tate. If it got out of control again, that is. Not that she expected it would. Tate wouldn't let that happen. He'd been clear about that.

Yet she had to wonder what the older couple would make of their separate bedrooms. Before the wedding, that might not have been a concern. After the wedding, it would be clear that she and Tate were having problems.

Not that it was anyone's business but their own.

Fifteen minutes later, Gemma walked into the sunroom. Nathan sat in his high chair, next to Tate, and the two of them looked so right together that she wanted to rush forward and be part of their family unit. She restrained herself as she kissed her darling son's head, then sat down beside them.

"You've done well," she told Tate, referring to the finger of toast Nathan chewed on.

"I can't take credit for that. It was Peggy's idea."

Just then Peggy came into the sunroom with a pot of coffee, and they chatted for a short time before she left. Gemma poured herself some cereal and crunched on that while keeping an eye on Nathan, and while trying *not* to keep an eye on Tate.

"He's a slow eater today, isn't he?" Tate said, after a couple of minutes.

All at once Gemma realized Tate was restless. She gave him a knowing look. "You're waiting to show him the sandbox, aren't you?"

His eyes filled with wry amusement. "Am I that obvious?"

"Yes," she teased. He chuckled, and the low sound softened the tension between them.

Thankfully, Nathan threw his remaining finger of toast on the floor right then. By the time she'd picked it up and discarded it, she hoped she could blame her flushed cheeks on having to bend down to the floor.

Tate got to his feet. "I'd say he's finished eating, don't you think?"

She needn't have worried about explaining her flushed cheeks. Tate evidently had other priorities. "Just let me take him upstairs and change him out of his pajamas first."

Tate nodded. "I'll be outside. Don't be too long." He sauntered out toward the patio area.

Men!

Her heart actually felt lighter as she changed Nathan into jeans and a T-shirt. Their son may have been the reason for their marriage, but he was proving to be a great leveler, too.

Once back downstairs, Gemma found not only Tate outside at the sandbox, but Clive and Peggy, as well. Tate saw her coming and immediately took his son. The males joined right in with enthusiasm. Soon both men were kneeling on the grass outside the shell-shaped sandbox, not seeming to mind about their trousers, while Nathan sat in the middle of the sand, trying to grab the dump truck that Tate was showing him how to use.

Then Clive said something and Tate laughed. He was totally relishing being a father, Gemma mused, admitting she was seeing a new side to Tate. He treated Clive as a personal friend rather than an employee. He treated Peggy more like a mother figure. Gemma hadn't seen him with other people during their month together, but she'd assumed he would keep his distance because of who he was and especially with the hired help, but that wasn't the case.

"You should join them," Peggy encouraged.

Gemma looked down at her casual slacks and top that would have cost more than her weekly wage. "I'm not exactly dressed for it."

"Neither are they," Peggy pointed out with bemusement.

Gemma smiled. "They're having too much fun playing at being boys. I'll just watch for now."

Peggy nodded. "Well, I think I'll leave them to it. I must clean up the breakfast dishes."

As Gemma watched Tate be so caring and tender with his son, she suddenly felt herself blinking back tears. It must be the strain of the past two weeks, she decided, and turned to go inside.

By the time she entered the kitchen where Peggy was busy cleaning, she was fine. She poured herself a cup of coffee. "Can I pour you a cup, too, Peggy?"

The older woman looked up from stacking the dishwasher. "No, thanks, Gemm…I mean, Mrs. Chandler."

Gemma only now realized the housekeeper hadn't addressed her by name since the wedding yesterday. "Gemma will do nicely, Peggy. Otherwise I may not know who you're talking to."

"But you're Mrs. Chandler now," Peggy said, not looking as if she would be swayed.

"And I was Miss Watkins these past ten days and you didn't have a problem calling me Gemma then." She had insisted right from the start, and while Peggy had been a little reluctant at first, she'd agreed to use Gemma's first name in private.

"I know, but that was then and this is now."

"That doesn't make sense, Peggy," she teased.

"It does to me. Mr. Chandler is Mr. Chandler, and you're Mrs. Chandler."

Gemma laughingly held up a hand. "You're making my head spin."

Peggy wrinkled her nose. "It does seem silly, but please, allow me this."

Gemma remembered how the other woman had mentioned Tate telling them to call him by his first name but they had refused, not because they didn't like him but because they were old-fashioned.

"Okay, I give in." Gemma paused deliberately. "For now."

The housekeeper clucked her tongue with mild exasperation as she continued clearing up. "How are you feeling now that the wedding's over?"

"Relieved," Gemma quipped, then hoped she didn't sound like she was all about getting married to a rich man. "I mean, relieved that the day is finally over. It was quite nerve-racking."

Peggy nodded, her eyes understanding. "Getting married is more wearing on the nerves than not. My eldest daughter was a complete wreck. She even fainted at the altar."

"*Who* fainted at the altar?" Tate said, coming into the kitchen with Nathan on his hip.

"That would be Sonya," Clive joked, following him. "Our eldest daughter. She's a bit of a drama queen."

"Clive," Peggy admonished, easing into a smile. "He's right, though. She *is* a drama queen."

"That girl is never going to change. She's thirty now and still doing it." Clive shook his head as he walked over to the refrigerator. "What's that old saying about a leopard not changing its spots?"

As if he couldn't help himself, Tate's eyes shot to Gemma. He looked away again as fast, but she didn't need three guesses to know he was thinking about her supposed kiss with his best friend.

"And you love her anyway," Peggy pointed out to her husband.

Clive grinned. "Of course."

Peggy returned the smile, then turned her attention to Nathan. "Heavens, what did you two do to that young fellow? He looks like he's been sandblasted."

Tate finally focused on the housekeeper. "He kept trying to eat the sand, so we've brought him in to show him the new activity center."

"They're a handful at this age," Peggy said.

Nathan was the excuse Gemma needed. She moved to collect him from Tate's arms. "I'd better take him upstairs for a wash first."

Tate handed Nathan over without a word and she made her escape. But not before she'd seen the look in her husband's eyes. He considered her a person who would never change for the better. A person worthy of his mistrust. It was just a pity he couldn't see how inflexible he was being himself.

Surprisingly, later that day they did go for that drive, and Tate was polite but remote, as if he'd been reminded of exactly who his wife was and regretted getting close to her earlier. He was the same for the rest of the week, whether they went sightseeing or lazed about on the patio with Nathan or watched television together after dinner. The only time he'd said anything the least personal to her was when she'd been lounging on the deck chair, immersed in a book.

"Don't stay out here too long in the sun or you'll get burned," he'd warned, startling her as he'd stepped onto the patio.

She looked up at the sky, noting the sun was overhead. "I was in the shade before."

"Yes, but the sun's moved."

He went back inside.

And that was that.

He'd done his duty.

Then, halfway through Friday morning, Gemma was about to leave her room when she caught sight of the light flashing on the telephone beside the bed. Nathan was asleep in his crib. Tate and Clive were in the garage checking on a problem with Clive's car. The sound of the vacuum cleaner came from another part of the house and she knew Peggy couldn't hear the telephone ringing. Thinking it might be important, Gemma picked up the handset, almost dropping it again at the sound of the male voice on the other end of the line.

"Well, well," Drake Fulton's voice said into the black hole that suddenly swallowed her up. "If it isn't Gemma Watkins…oops, it's Gemma Chandler now, isn't it?"

He sounded pleasant enough, if anyone had been listening on another extension, but she knew there was more than that in his voice. "What do you want, Drake?"

"Congratulations are in order, I believe. A marriage *and* a son. Well done, Gem."

She clasped the phone tighter. She hated him calling her Gem. He only ever did that in private. "Are you looking for Tate?"

"I was." He didn't acknowledge her abrupt tone. "I wanted to apologize again for not being able to make the wedding, but I thought it best I didn't go. Tate agreed with me that it was the right thing to do…under the circumstances."

Gemma had to bite her tongue. This man didn't know how to do the right thing, under any circumstances. "I'll tell Tate you called."

"No need," he said cheerily. "I'll phone him back another time."

"Goodbye, Drake." She hung up with shaking fingers and sank down on the bed, thoughts milling in her head. Drake hadn't called to talk to Tate at all. He'd called on the off-chance that *she* might answer the phone, otherwise he could have easily called Tate on his cell phone.

Gemma had to get out of the room and out of the house. She jumped to her feet, sick to her stomach. "I'm going for a walk to the lake," she told Peggy as calmly as she could when she passed her vacuuming downstairs. "Would you keep an eye on Nathan? He should sleep for another hour or so."

"Of course."

"Thanks. I just need some fresh air." She needed to get the stink of Drake Fulton out of her mind.

Gemma was still upset when she reached the sanctuary of the lake, where the cluster of trees and the gazebo hid her from view. She sank down on a small bench near the water's edge. There was no way she could tell Tate about the call. He'd accuse her of somehow engineering this so she could talk to Drake. How she could have achieved that she didn't know, but Tate was blind where she was concerned and totally biased about his best friend.

God, she couldn't even confide how ill at ease Drake had made her, or Tate would say she was imagining things or, worse, trying to stir up more trouble. Hadn't she once attempted to tell him how Drake had made her uncomfortable? He hadn't been prepared to listen then and she was sure he wouldn't now. Otherwise he'd already know that this was the way Drake worked, pretending to be friendly in front of others, pretending to be Tate's best friend, while trying to get her into bed.

No doubt if she'd fallen for Drake's charms and slept with him two years ago he'd have dumped her as quickly as Tate had. He hadn't liked that she'd ignored his advances then, and she could tell he still didn't like it. How far would he go now that she was married to Tate and had a child? She suspected he wouldn't stop at less than destroying what she and Tate had. Suddenly her tenuous hold on her marriage was everything to her. She didn't want to lose it.

Right then, a horse and rider came over the rise and Gemma groaned, wishing she'd gone somewhere else. Wasn't there anywhere she could have some privacy in this place? The last thing she wanted right now was company.

Rolly saw her and waved, then brought the horse in her direction. "I didn't think I'd see you here this morning," he said as he got closer.

She rose to her feet and mustered up a smile. "It was too nice to stay inside."

"I'm later than usual. I had to do a job for my dad." He slid down to the ground and smoothed his hand along the horse's flank as he spoke to her. "Where's your son?"

"He's back at the house, but Tate will be bringing him down to see the swans soon."

"Does he like the swans?" he said, looking a bit preoccupied as he dropped the reins and let the horse amble over to the water's edge.

"Yes, he does." There was a momentary lull. "Rolly, is something the matter?"

Indecision crossed his face, then, "My dad wants me to go visit my mother."

She should have known it would be a family problem. There didn't seem to be any other kind right now.

She felt sorry for the teenager. He'd been nice to her, and helping him would certainly stop her from thinking about her own problems. "You don't want to visit her?"

He shrugged. "She married someone else, but I don't like him much."

"Why not?"

"He doesn't want me there. He just wants my mom."

Gemma totally understood not being wanted, and her heart squeezed for him. "I wish I could tell you it shouldn't be like that, but sometimes no matter how much we wish for something, it still doesn't happen." She didn't want him to feel too down about it all, though. "But I have absolutely no doubt you'll get through it."

A spark of hope brightened his eyes. "Really?"

"Really. And think about how happy it will make your mother if you visit her," she said. It would be wonderful if her own mother would be as happy, but Gemma knew that wasn't about to happen.

The teenager gazed at her speculatively. "You know a lot about life and things, don't you?"

"No more than anyone else."

Suddenly, he looked at the top of her head. "Hey, you've got something in your hair." He took a couple of steps forward and reached to pick it off. "It's only a gum leaf. I get them in my hair all—"

"Gemma," Tate's voice snapped behind them.

Gemma spun around at the same time as Rolly did. "Tate!" she exclaimed, feeling her cheeks instantly flush with a heat she had no control over.

A guilty flush, Tate decided, unable to believe this was happening again. Peggy had told him she'd gone for a walk down here, but this was more than that. This was a rendezvous.

No wonder she'd put Nathan to bed. Was no man—no *boy*—safe from his wife? Did she need male attention all the time, no matter what the age of the cohort? Their marriage wasn't a bed of roses right now, but couldn't she at least remain faithful while they were still on their honeymoon?

Clearly not.

"Er...where's Nathan?" she asked, as if she was trying to smooth things over. "I thought you were bringing him down here to see the swans."

Tate knew that was an outright lie, but he leashed his immediate reaction. What was between him and Gemma stayed between him and Gemma. "He's still sleeping."

"Hi, Tate," Rolly said, a slight flush to his cheeks that told Tate more than he wanted to know. "Long time, no see."

Tate gave a short nod in acknowledgment. "Rolly."

The teenager looked at Gemma then nervously back at Tate. "I was just letting the horse drink from the lake. Your grandfather told me I could."

"I know."

"So...you don't mind if I continue that?"

"No, I don't mind." The kid was pretending he was

nervous over bringing the horse here, when they both knew that was just an excuse.

"Great. Thanks." Rolly picked up the reins and scampered up on the horse. "I'd better be getting back or my dad will come looking for me." He glanced at Gemma and gave a quick smile. "Thanks, Gemma."

It was just as well the teenager took off after that. Tate gritted his teeth. God, how could he have been so stupid as to let his guard down with her? Gemma was beautiful, but she wouldn't turn him into a fool again.

"Tate—"

"I don't want to hear it, Gemma." He stepped forward and put his hand under her elbow, intending to walk her back to the house.

She took a couple of steps with him, then pulled away. "You're overreacting."

"Am I?" He didn't think so. How could he forget what had happened with Drake?

"Rolly was merely getting a leaf out of my hair."

He gave her a skeptical look. "Is that what you call it these days?"

"Don't be ridiculous," she said dismissively, sending his blood pressure soaring.

His jaw clenched tight. "How long has this been going on?"

"Nothing's going on," she snapped, but she had turned pale. "I met Rolly by accident the other day when I brought Nathan down here. This is only the second time I've run into him."

"Why did he thank you then? *What* did he thank you for?"

She shrugged. "He's got some personal problems. I was helping him sort them out."

"Yeah, I could see that." Tate let his voice drip with sarcasm.

She drew herself up taller, looking haughty and so darn beautiful. "Don't you dare suggest anything else, Tate Chandler. He's a boy who needed to talk and that's all."

Was she blind? "He's only ten years younger than you. He's a young man with a young man's hormones, and having you close by would be torture for him." Dammit, she was torturing *him*.

"And that's got to appeal to me, does it? A pimply teenager with raging hormones is just what I've been waiting for. Gosh, all my Christmases have come at once. I don't know how I've contained my excitement all this time."

He grimaced. Okay, so she had a point. Perhaps he could admit his reaction had been over the top. But seeing the young man touch her hair—he'd felt as if he was losing her again, as crazy as that sounded. Last time, he'd decided it had been for good, but this time he *knew* it would be forever. Not even for Nathan's sake would he go through that again. Hell, if she had any affairs in the future—and God help her if she did—then it would be *for* Nathan's sake they would split up.

He didn't want it to get that far. "Just stay away from Rolly."

She crossed her arms over her firm breasts. "You know what? I don't have to do a thing you tell me to do."

For some reason the image of her breasts took precedence. And suddenly Rolly wasn't the problem. "You never did do anything I told you to do. But you're my wife now, so perhaps you'd best learn."

"Then perhaps *you* should act like I'm your wife."

The comment threw him. "What does that mean?"

"You figure it out."

Was she suggesting what he thought she was suggesting? "If you're feeling lonely, find another outlet. Don't go turning to someone else."

"Well, it's no use turning to you, is it, Tate?"

Something burst inside him.

He slipped his hand under her hair and drew her hard against his body. She gasped as he held her head still, his lips seeking and finding hers, taking advantage of her open mouth and sliding his tongue straight in and over the top of hers, instinctively wanting to dominate her. Hell, he wanted to erase the kiss of another man—*any* man—right out of her mouth.

Then she came alive and seized control. Suddenly *she* was the one calling the shots, and he was the one being taken over. She made him remember what their kisses had been like—*real* kisses, *no-holds-barred* kisses—as she arched against him and sent the blood storming through his veins, his muscles locking into place, his body tightening with need against her softness.

A buzzing sound interrupted his consciousness.

For a moment he didn't realize what it was, but soon the sound of a small, low-flying plane could be heard coming closer. Breaking off the kiss, he shielded Gemma and moved her a few feet to the side of the gazebo and out of sight. He wouldn't let anyone see them. This was private property.

The plane didn't appear to be scouring the area. It was heading in a direct line north, so it was unlikely to be reporters. He waited until it was past the house before looking at her.

For a long moment, he was riveted by her and what had just passed between them. Had he really ever been convinced he wouldn't let himself be tempted by her charms? Heaven help him, but his body still thrummed with need as he noted the color high in her cheeks and her softly swollen lips. Her eyes were uncertain now, calling to something inside him. Thankfully sanity prevailed. Giving in would be a mistake.

Just like *she* had made a mistake when she'd kissed his best friend, he reminded himself.

"I won't be a substitute, dammit," he said, dragging up the thought of her and Drake together to get him through this moment. He had to. He had to protect himself from his own desires.

She drew in a sharp breath. "Tate—"

"You'd better go back to the house."

"But—"

"Just go."

She looked like she might say something further, but she merely glared at him before hurrying along the path.

Tate ran his fingers through his hair, damn grateful she had gone. The memory of her and Drake kissing might be in his mind, but it was a different memory beating through his body right now. He had to take her to his bed or learn to live with the wanting.

Neither option was acceptable.

Gemma's mind was reeling as she straightened her blouse and hurried back to the house. How could Tate think he was a substitute for any man? No one else had ever come close to him.

And while he had carried on about Rolly, it had been a storm in a teacup. The real issue was Drake. Even when she and Tate had good moments between them, it always came back to the other man. Drake had been the cause of their breakup. Drake was the reason for her walk today, which had resulted in that kiss just now. And coming full circle, Drake was the cause of Tate's contempt for her.

Yet in spite of Drake, there was still something between her and Tate that wouldn't be denied. She was horrified with herself for challenging him to kiss her like she had. She didn't know where the words had come from, but she should have remembered that he always faced a challenge.

Lord, as much as she'd wanted Tate to kiss her, she wished he hadn't. It only made her more aware of what she *couldn't* have and of what she *shouldn't* be wanting. Now every time she was with Tate, and even when she wasn't, there would be this consciousness between them.

Already she ached to be back in his arms.

She didn't expect him to come to her room a short time later and tell her they were going back to the city tomorrow.

"Won't that cause suspicion?" she asked with a frown.

"It's only a day early. I don't think it'll matter." A pulse began beating in his cheekbone. "And we ignore what happened before, right?"

"For how long, Tate?" she heard herself ask.

"For as long as it takes."

"To do what? To convince yourself I'm worthy of your touch?"

"A bit of honesty wouldn't go amiss."

"So if I tell you I kissed Drake on purpose then you'll forgive me and we'll be able to move on?"

His eyes flared with triumph. "I'm not making any promises, but I'll try."

Her heart gave a painful twist. "How noble of you. Sorry, but I'm not telling a lie just so you can feel better about something that's simply not true."

He expelled a raspy breath. "Nothing was ever simple between us, Gemma."

She wasn't getting through to him. So there was nothing left to do but to salvage her pride. "Actually, I thought that's all we ever had between us—*simple* lust."

His mouth tightened. "It was…until you wanted Drake."

He left the room and Gemma sank down on the bed, a sob catching in her throat. It was like talking to a brick wall. What could she do now but keep right on doing what she was already doing, knowing she had done nothing wrong in the first place.

It was the only way to make this marriage work.

Six

Late the next morning, Peggy and Clive left the mansion an hour before them and drove back to Melbourne in their own car. By the time Tate and Gemma arrived, a light lunch had already been prepared.

Nathan had slept nearly the whole way, so now he was a ball of energy and very fidgety as Gemma helped him eat his lunch. He was going to keep her on her toes for the rest of the day, she knew, and perhaps that wasn't a bad thing. Without a doubt, Tate would head to his study and throw himself into his work, or even go into his office in the city. It would be business as usual for him from now on.

The job.

Play with his son.

Ignore her.

"What are you doing for the rest of the afternoon?" he asked, as if reading her thoughts.

"I'm not sure." She could easily have taken a nap, but hopefully she'd get her second wind soon. She hadn't had time for naps when she'd been working, she reminded herself. "I might take Nathan for a walk to the local shops."

Tate frowned. "What do you need? Clive can get it for you. Just ask."

She lifted a shoulder and then let it drop. "I don't need anything really. It's merely something to do to help Nathan chew up some energy."

His lips twisted. "I see. You're sick of all this already, are you?"

"No." Why did he turn her words around? "I merely thought Nathan might like some fresh air, that's all. It's no different from me taking him down to the lake." She could have bit her tongue off when Tate's jaw clenched tight.

"I'll come with you."

Her eyebrows shot up. "Why?"

"Because."

"I see. You think I'll leave Nathan sitting in his stroller while some store owner has his way with me out back, do you?"

Tate cursed low. "I'm coming with you and that's that. We'll go through a side entrance in case any reporters are out front. Put sun hats on you both. And wear your sunglasses."

He was serious about coming with them. "All that for a short walk?"

"A short walk could turn into a nightmare if the reporters discover us."

Thoughts of cameras being pushed in Nathan's face turned her cold. "On second thought, it's probably best not to go."

"We're not prisoners, Gemma. We'll go out and get our son an ice cream if we want. No one is going to stop us."

Understanding dawned. She had to admit, when she thought about it some more, she felt the same. This was Australia, for heaven's sake. Surely they were entitled to some space to themselves? Still, she'd feel better with Tate there to protect them.

After that, considering everything between them, it was quite an enjoyable walk in the sunshine. Tate hadn't worn a hat, but he seemed to relax more with each step, and so did she. They even stopped at a local park next to the small strip of shops so she could feed Nathan some ice cream.

It was Saturday, so there were quite a few people in the park. A couple of children playing with a small puppy caught Nathan's attention, and he started to laugh at their antics. The children, a girl and a boy around seven or eight, heard him and brought the puppy over. Before they knew it, the puppy was licking drops of ice cream off Nathan's T-shirt.

Gemma actually felt happy—seriously happy—as Tate asked about the children's names and the age of the puppy. He was really good with the kids.

A nice-looking man strolled toward them from the direction of the shops, carrying a loaf of bread. "I hope they aren't bothering you," he said, smiling as he approached.

Tate smiled back. "Not at all. They've been keeping us quite entertained."

The man blinked, and Gemma knew he'd recognized Tate. So much for their sunglasses and her sun hat!

"If you want to wear your kids out, just get them a puppy," the man joked.

"I plan on it, when my son's a little older." Tate proudly glanced at Nathan.

A short time later, the other family left and Gemma couldn't help saying something. "Did you mean it about getting Nathan a dog?"

"Sure, why not?" Tate lifted a brow. "You don't want him to have one?"

"No, I think it's a great idea." She shrugged. "It's just such a…family thing to do."

An odd expression flickered across his face. "We *are* a family now," he said, as he turned away to push the stroller.

Her vision blurred and she was thankful for her sunglasses. She didn't want to acknowledge how much his words meant to her, but his comment warmed her all the way home.

On their return, Gemma carried Nathan into the informal living room while Tate put the stroller away. She vaguely heard Peggy's voice, but she didn't take much notice as she placed Nathan down on the carpet and let him crawl around the now-childproof room.

About ten minutes later Tate came through the doorway, sheets of paper in his hands, his face tight. He held them out toward her. "Someone's just posted these on the internet," he said, keeping his voice low. All his earlier softness had disappeared.

She frowned as she read what was in her hands, then gasped, her eyes widening. On one page was a photograph of her old apartment minus the furniture. The place looked like it needed a coat of paint and seemed a little shabby. On another was a picture of Tate's house, with its magnificent gardens and luxury cars parked in the sweeping driveway. Farther, on the next page, someone had put the two together with the caption, "From *This* to *This* in Two Weeks," then there were some derogatory remarks, not about Tate but about her becoming pregnant on purpose so she could marry into money.

She lifted her head in bewilderment, trying to get her head around it all. "*This* is on the internet?"

"Yes."

"But why?" She swallowed hard, her mind whirring. "How did you even know these were there?"

"One of Bree's friends rang to tell her about it, so naturally my sister rang here. She left a message with Peggy." Something brutal entered his eyes. "I printed them up to show you. I'll get my lawyer to investigate the website."

The thought of this being all over the internet turned her stomach. "Investigate?"

"I'll find out who's done this. They'll pay."

She took a shuddering breath. "God, I feel violated." Not only was her reputation being ripped to shreds in a public forum, but the place—the *home*—she'd tried to make for her and Nathan had been held up for everyone to see—and judge.

She felt tears mist her eyes. Could her day—her *life*— get any worse? She was so emotionally drained. As one of the Chandlers now, did she have it in her to take this over all the years ahead?

"Gemma?"

She turned her back on him and blinked rapidly, seeing her son playing on the carpet with his toys but more aware of Tate. She didn't want this man to see her crying. It would be the last straw for her. She had to remain strong, or fall in a heap.

"Gemma?" he said, more softly this time.

She remembered something. She spun back. "The humanitarian award! This might ruin it." A sob escaped her lips. "Oh, God, I seem to be wrecking your family's chances everywhere I turn."

"Screw the award."

"Wh-what?"

"I said screw the award. This attack on you is more important. I won't have your character denigrated in such a personal way like this. You're my wife now, and as such you should have respect." His head at a proud angle, he took the papers out of her hand and strode to the door, purpose in every tense line of his shoulders, his intention obvious.

Don't mess with his family.

Okay, so it wasn't about *her* exactly. It was more about her position and probably more for Nathan's sake than not. But that didn't change something quite remarkable: Tate wasn't blaming her for this.

And that had to be a first.

The rest of the day went by quietly and Gemma wasn't unhappy about that. Except for dinner and time spent with his son, Tate stayed in his study, no doubt checking into this latest mess.

He didn't mention anything more about it the next morning when she went down to breakfast, so Gemma didn't either. Perhaps if he played with Nathan after breakfast, she might go into his study to check online. But, she decided, that would only upset her. Best to let Tate handle it. He had the means and the connections to get to the bottom of it fast.

Then over breakfast he said, "I've given Peggy and Clive the rest of the day off so they can visit their grandchildren." He paused. "And my parents have invited us to lunch."

Gemma groaned inwardly. The one place she *didn't* want to be today was with his family. His mother was nice, but the rest of them hadn't forgiven her for keeping Nathan from his birthright. Now they would have something more to castigate her about.

"They usually eat a late lunch," he continued, "so we won't have to leave until around one. That will give Nathan time for his morning nap."

"Er…did you tell them about the photos?"

"I didn't have to. Bree already told them."

"How kind."

He gave her a sharp look. "My sister was only trying to look after them."

Gemma understood that, but it was at *her* expense. "And?"

"They want to get to the bottom of it as much as we do."

She noticed he didn't say anything about them not blaming *her* for bringing more ill-repute on their family name.

"Let it go for now, Gemma. There's nothing we can do at the moment. I've got someone working on it, and we'll find the culprit as fast as we can."

He was right. She tried to relax. "At least they weren't nude photographs," she quipped, then froze. What on earth had made her say that?

"Should we be worried about that?" he demanded.

"Of course not!" She'd never been promiscuous with her favors. *Except with him.* But she refused to look away. She had nothing to be ashamed of. Not with him, not with anyone.

They glared eye-to-eye, then something lifted in his gaze and she could see he believed her. Before she could shake off the moment, she realized he was mentally undressing her, just like he used to…right down to her bare skin…sending her stomach into a flutter. Then he noticed her noticing, and he looked away, breaking the connection.

Thankfully Peggy came in then, but it took a while before Gemma's pulse settled to its normal pace. After breakfast, she took the opportunity to escape, carrying Nathan upstairs to pick out an outfit for him to wear to lunch while Tate answered a call on his cell phone.

The morning passed surprisingly quickly. She brought Nathan back downstairs, but Tate's study door was firmly closed. She kept busy, playing with Nathan on the carpet.

Then her eye caught sight of a local newspaper. She jumped to her feet, panic spurting through her veins. Could the story have reached the newspapers? She left Nathan to play close by with his toys while she sat on the sofa and combed the pages, shuddering with relief when she didn't find anything. Even so, how long could that last?

Shrugging aside a growing sense of despondency over it all, Gemma eventually took Nathan back upstairs for a mid-morning nap. He cried a little in resistance, but if he was going to be awake all afternoon then he needed some sleep first. A couple of minutes later he was out like a light.

She'd just put on a dress and was finishing her makeup in preparation for the luncheon, when Tate knocked on her door. He always knocked before entering now, except that time the newspapers had called his father and broke the news about Nathan. Tate had been angry enough to walk right in then.

"Your parents are here," he said without preamble.

The closed tube of lipstick slipped from her fingers and onto the vanity. "My pa-parents?"

His gaze sharpened. "The guard rang from the front gate. I knew who they were as soon as I saw them on the security camera. You once showed me a photograph, remember?"

"Oh, my God," she muttered, her mind agog. Her parents were *here?* They were back from their Mediterranean cruise? They *wanted* to see her?

"I told them to wait."

She blinked. "You did?"

"I didn't know if you wanted to see them or not." He left a longish pause. "Do you?"

Did she?

"I'm not sure," she admitted, then realized he'd seen more than she knew when a frown creased his forehead.

"Do I let them in, Gemma? You have to make a decision. I can tell them to go away or—"

She couldn't bear that. "No, let them in."

He stared a moment more as if judging her sincerity, then, satisfied, he walked over to the bedside table and used the telephone to talk to the security guard.

Gemma stood there, still reeling from the news. This didn't seem real. She'd wanted their support for so long... yearned for them to ask to see her and Nathan. She could admit that to herself now.

He hung up the phone. "Right, they're on the way."

The words somehow pulled her together, reminding her that this was her problem, not Tate's. It was best she handle it herself. And she had to admit she was a little ashamed for him to know what had happened with her parents. Was loving a daughter through thick and thin so very difficult?

She veiled her expression. "Thank you, Tate. I'd like to see them alone."

"No."

"Tate—"

"What's going on with you and them anyway? I know there's something wrong, so don't tell me there isn't."

"I'll tell you later. There's no time right now."

"There's time enough to give me the gist of it."

She deliberately hadn't told him what had transpired, not wanting him to tap into her emotions and use her pain against her. Now she knew that was one thing he wouldn't do, at least where her parents were concerned. He valued family too much. And while she didn't want his sympathy, she wanted him on her side. She needed his support right now, if only for this short time.

She took a shuddering breath, the words harder to say than she'd expected. "If you really want to know, they kicked me out when I told them I was pregnant."

Rage erupted in his eyes. "What the hell! God, what type of parents do that sort of thing?"

She wasn't totally sure if the rage was for her or for his son. "They couldn't handle the shame of their daughter being pregnant and unmarried." She tried to sound uncaring, but it still hurt deeply that her mother and father had turned their backs on her when she'd needed them most.

And on their grandson.

Tate's jaw flexed. "Shame on *them*."

Something softened inside her. "Thank you," she whispered, then drew her shoulders back. It was time to move.

"Gemma, look, I'd fully understand if you don't want to see them."

She appreciated the turnabout. "No, it's best this way." Otherwise she'd always wonder why they'd come. Besides, she needed to think about Nathan. If there was a chance they wanted their grandson in their lives, she couldn't deny him that opportunity. Anyway, once they saw Nathan they would fall in love with him. She was certain of that.

For all her self-assurance, when she and Tate reached the bottom of the stairs, she hesitated. She saw their shadows through the glass door and was unable to bring herself to open it. Reminiscent of their wedding day, when they'd had to face the reporters outside, Tate gave her shoulder a squeeze. Then he moved forward.

She quickly grasped his arm. "They're really not so bad, Tate." She didn't want him to think it was *all* their fault. For good or bad, she *had* made some unwise choices.

He nodded but his face closed up. And then he opened the door. Gemma stood where she was as he introduced himself and invited her parents inside. They saw her and hesitated before stepping into the foyer. Her heart staggered beneath her breast. Was it too much to hope that they might have rushed forward and taken her in their arms?

On second thought, perhaps they were simply over-whelmed, she told herself, not willing to let the doubt-devils get to her this early. She went to them and kissed them on their cheeks. "Mom. Dad. It's lovely to see you both." But she noticed her mother had stiffened at Gemma's touch.

"Hello, Gemma," Meryl Watkins said without a hint of warmth. She'd always spoken like that, Gemma reminded herself.

Her father's expression faltered before he cleared his throat. Frank Watkins had always given in to her mother, even if Gemma sensed he didn't always agree with her. "Yes, hello, Gemma."

There was an awkward silence. It was like they were strangers. She waited for them to ask about Nathan, then was disappointed when they simply stood there.

"Let's go to the drawing room," Tate suggested.

"Yes, good idea." Gemma tried hard to relax. "Would you like some coffee or tea?"

"No, thank you, Gemma." Her mother walked through the arched doorway, looking critically around the room before sitting down on the sofa without being asked. "This is certainly very nice, don't you think, Frank?"

Her father nodded as he placed himself beside her mother. "You've done well for yourself, Gemma."

Gemma ignored the tightening of Tate's mouth as she moved to sit opposite them. "I hear you've been on a Mediterranean cruise."

Her father's bushy eyebrows knitted together. "How did you know that?"

"When no one answered the phone at home, I phoned your work. I wanted to invite you to the wedding." Hopefully they would see that as a peace offering.

Frank glanced at his wife. "See, I told you she would have sent an invitation."

Gemma wasn't sure she liked being called "she" in such a fashion. Couldn't her own father call her by her first name?

And were they ever going to ask about Nathan?

"The papers said it was a lovely wedding," her mother said. "Though Gemma," her tone turned disapproving now, "I really don't think you should have worn white."

The criticism stung, but Gemma tried to move past the hurt, for Nathan's sake. "That's a bit old-fashioned, isn't it, Mom?" she teased, trying to lighten the mood.

"And I raised you to be an old-fashioned girl," her mother said, then gave a heavy sigh. "Still, at least you're married now."

Disillusionment ripped through Gemma. She was beginning to see that nothing had changed. It had been hard growing up under constant disapproval. It was the reason she had moved out once she'd found herself a decent job. Her parents hadn't tried to dissuade her, and she'd had the feeling they'd been relieved to get her out of the house. It had been the same when she'd told them she was pregnant. She was too much of a problem for them. They couldn't cope, so they'd been happy to get her out of their lives.

Tate had been standing by the large windows, but now he moved in closer, his eyes narrowing. "So the only reason you came to see Gemma now is because she's married?"

Her mother's face showed that she clearly didn't like Tate's tone. "That and because we wanted to see our grandson."

"Whom you haven't asked about," he pointed out.

"Give us time," her father tried to joke.

Tate came to stand by the sofa, intimidating as he looked down at the older pair. "I'd imagine that would be one of the first things *I'd* ask about."

"Of course you would," Frank said, his tone placating. "He's your son. We're only his grandparents."

Tate's eyebrows shot up. "Only? That about says it all, doesn't it?"

"I didn't mean it like that."

"And that's the real shame of it," Tate said, and a split second later he indicated the door with a brief dip of his head. "I'll see you both out now."

There was a stunned silence.

For a few seconds no one moved.

In spite of everything, Gemma was dismayed by what was happening. She'd didn't want it to end like this. It had hurt so much the last time they'd walked away from her.

"Are you going to let him talk to us this way?" Meryl Watkins demanded of her daughter.

Put on the spot, Gemma's mind stumbled. She'd tried

over and over to stand up to her mother, but she had always felt intimidated. In the end, it had been better to leave home. "Er...Tate has a point," she said, not daring to look directly at him, knowing what he would be thinking. But he had to understand there was something so...final about all this.

The older woman got to her feet. "The only point your husband has made is that he's kicking us out of his house."

"*Our* house," Tate corrected. "Mine and Gemma's house. And our son's."

"Come on, Frank. It's clear we're not wanted here."

Tate's mouth turned sour. "Good God, I don't believe you two. You haven't seen your daughter for more than a year, yet you both came in here without giving her a hug or a kiss. And you didn't even mention your grandson. So I have to ask myself why you're here at all." He scanned the pair, then a steely look entered his eyes. "I suspect you've been shamed into this by your friends. Is that what this is all about?"

As if he'd touched a nerve, her mother reddened. "How dare you!"

"I dare."

Suddenly Gemma knew that's exactly what this visit was about. Their daughter had married into a prominent family, and they were frightened they wouldn't look good in front of their friends. After all, if Gemma could catch a man like Tate Chandler, then perhaps she wasn't so terrible...

"You'll regret this, *Mr. Chandler,*" Meryl said now. "Your family's good name will be mud by the time we finish telling everyone how you stopped us from seeing our daughter and our grandson."

At the threat, Gemma finally found her mental footing.

For the first time in her life, she understood that she had done nothing to deserve the treatment her parents had dished out to her. Just like Nathan had done nothing wrong. Nor Tate. This battleground was all her parents' doing.

"Mom, while you're at it, don't forget to tell them how you and Dad turned your back on your unmarried, pregnant daughter, leaving me alone to fend for myself and my child."

Her mother pursed her lips. "You knew the rules."

"Rules?" Gemma scoffed. "Oh, yes, it's rules that matter to you, not me or your grandson."

Her father was shaking his head as he got to his feet. "Gemma, please, your mother doesn't mean—"

"Be quiet, Frank. I do mean it. Gemma has been nothing but a disappointment to us."

Gemma froze, vaguely aware of Tate's low curse. Just when she thought they couldn't do anything more to hurt her... She'd known she was a disappointment to them, but hearing it out loud like this...

As painful as it was, she wouldn't let them know just how much they'd hurt her. Her chin lifted. "At least I finally know what you think of me. Please leave. I never want to see either of you again."

Her mother's face didn't relent. She spun around and made for the front door, where Tate now stood sentry. Her father looked at her with a glimpse of compassion before he scurried after his wife.

Bitterness rose in Gemma's throat and bubbled over. "And by the way, Nathan is doing very nicely without either of you. So am I."

They left then, and Gemma collapsed on the sofa. She heard Tate close the front door, then heard car doors slam and her parents drive away. By the time Tate came back into the drawing room, she could feel a reaction setting in. This was it. She'd never see them again. The ties were finally cut.

She should feel relief.

She could only feel despair.

"I shouldn't have done that, Tate," she mumbled, hugging her arms around herself, trying to hold the pain in so that she wouldn't fall apart.

Sympathy shone from his eyes. "Don't do this to yourself, Gemma. They've treated you very badly."

She didn't want his sympathy. "Like *you've* treated me badly?"

His head went back.

"They're *my* parents, Tate," she said, getting to her feet, anger bubbling up inside her. She wanted to strike out, at anyone. He would do. "I should have told them to go in the first place."

He remained calm. "So why didn't you?"

She had to stay angry. Anger would get her through this. "I was thinking of Nathan. They're his grandparents."

"Pity they didn't act like it." He tilted his head at her. "Do you really want people like them in your son's life?"

"No, but it should have been *my* decision to ask them to go, not yours."

"I didn't think you would do it."

She lifted her chin. "You were wrong."

A heartbeat passed.

"I was proud of you, Gemma." His voice had softened.

Something wobbled inside her. "Don't say that."

"Why not?"

Tears weren't far away, but she held them back. "I'll cry. And I don't want to cry."

"I'd say you're more than entitled."

All at once she longed to have someone put their arms

around her and tell her everything would be okay. She'd never had anyone to reassure her in such a way.

And now her parents never would.

Through a haze of emotion she saw Tate. He was the only person who had ever made her feel safe. She needed to recapture that feeling. "Tate, make love to me."

Time seemed to decelerate.

"What?"

"Make love to me. Please. I need you."

He stiffened. "Gemma—"

The next second, she knew he would refuse. Her heart squeezed as she put on a brave face. "That's okay, I understand." She stepped past him, intending to rush to her room and lick her wounds. "My parents didn't want me, so I can't blame you for—"

He put his hand on her arm, stopping her. "Don't put me in the same category as them." He tugged her gently toward him. "Do I want you?" His eyes darkened. "Oh, yeah, I want you, Gemma."

The last thing she saw was Tate's head lowering, blocking out the sunlight streaming through the windows. Or was it dark because her eyelids had come down? She didn't know. She didn't care. The feel of his arms around her, the touch of his lips on hers, the raw emotion she'd heard in his voice—all of it cut away their surroundings. A breath caught in her throat.

The taste of him flooded her and she shuddered in pleasure. Her hands slid up and locked behind his neck, clinging to him as she gave him kiss for kiss. She couldn't believe she was finally in Tate's arms, and there was no denying that he wanted her. She could feel his arousal growing, hardening against her stomach.

His lips made their way along her jawline, and she let her head fall back to give him better access. He dallied briefly at her earlobe before his kisses moved to the sensitive skin of her neck. Eyes remaining shut, she felt him place his lips against the base of her throat and hold there for a few seconds. She held still, too.

Then his hand slid under her hair and eased her zipper down. The dress came off her shoulders with a gentle draft of air as he pushed the material down and let it descend to the carpet, leaving her in bra and panties.

Only then did she open her eyes. His gaze traveled over her body like a whisper. "You're even more beautiful now than before."

Her heart bounced. "I am?"

"You've had my baby," he said simply, but there was nothing simple about the way he brushed his fingers between her breasts to her trim stomach, making her quiver in reaction.

Then his fingers slipped inside one cup of her bra and lifted out her breast, holding it up for his pleasure. He captured her nipple with his mouth. She took quick breaths, hearing the sound reverberate inside her throat, growing tenfold as his tongue played with the tightening bud.

He caressed her other breast with his hands then his mouth, and soon her bra disappeared. Everything intensified. Her panties were gone. He pressed her down on the sofa and stretched her out on it. He slipped a cushion under her head, clearly concerned for her comfort, making her feel special even as the pressure built between them.

He moved back and stood looking down at her. "God, I want to take my time with you," he rasped, his blue eyes deepening with color.

Somewhere in the back of her mind she knew they had a luncheon to attend and a child to get ready, but it had been almost two long years since he'd been a part of her. And she couldn't bear it if Nathan were to wake up right now and put a stop to this. Would they ever get back to this moment? Their emotions were high, but nothing between them had been resolved…

"Next time," she whispered, beckoning him to join her, vaguely thankful they were the only adults in the house.

He proceeded to strip off his clothes. Her eyes followed every sinew revealed, every hair on his chest, the darker patch surrounding his full erection. He lowered himself down on her, but not in her. Not yet. They both knew the feel of him against her naked skin was just too much pleasure to sacrifice for the sake of time.

But soon it wasn't enough. He kissed her deeply, adjusting himself more fully, probing now at the top of her thighs. The air grew thick as she opened her legs. She wanted him to be a part of her. She'd missed him so much.

And then he stopped.

"Gemma?"

She looked into his eyes and saw something that would have made her knees buckle, if she'd been standing.

"You are *not* a disappointment to anyone."

Her heart rolled over, the breath locked in her throat. For him to take this moment to say that when he was more than ready to *take* her…

"Thank you," she whispered, grateful that no matter what had passed between them he had given her this.

"And you've *never* been a substitute for anyone else," she said, risking everything in the spirit of the moment, wanting him to remember how it had once been for them. It was important that he knew the truth.

His eyes flared, but she didn't give him time to speak.

She held on to his shoulders and tilted her lower body up to his. "I want *you,* Tate."

He groaned. It was a sound of need, but she wasn't sure if he would push into her or pull away. Did he need to get away from her? Or did he need her?

As if he couldn't stop himself, the next second he thrust between her thighs. Her heart soared and she rose to meet him. He groaned again and she knew she was what he needed, at least right now. He thrust deeper and she clung to him as he took her higher.

"Only you," she whispered, then she shattered around him, feeling him climax inside her.

Tate kissed Gemma hard and quick, then moved away to gather her clothes and hand them to her. He began pulling on his own clothes, needing to keep himself busy and not look at her naked body lying there all delicious and warm from his touch. He could take her again right now.

Easily.

He waited until he was dressed before looking down at her again. "Are you okay?"

She had sat up to dress, and now she gave a small smile. "Sure."

He searched her eyes, but she wasn't giving anything away, and he wasn't about to either. "We'll leave for lunch in an hour," he said, and left the room. He had to walk away before he was tempted to carry her upstairs and tumble her on his bed.

He was growing hard just thinking about it. Her sexual power over him was immense. Hell, he hadn't even given a thought to contraception. They'd deal with that later. There were already too many complications between him and Gemma.

If he were to be truthful, their lovemaking had been

about more than the sexual pull she had over him. A combination of things had been building since their marriage. First Rolly, though Tate had to admit he'd been in the wrong about the teenager. Then the pictures on the internet showing Gemma's threadbare apartment and hinting she was a gold digger. Yesterday, the puppy and Gemma asking if they could have a dog, as if she'd accepted they were now a family.

But all that paled in comparison to her parents' visit. And what a piece of work they were! Learning what they had done to her, seeing how they'd treated her today, had caused a primitive anger to well up inside him. He'd gone hot with rage, then ice cold. Gemma had made him proud that she'd stood up to them.

And him.

And then she'd blown him away when she'd asked him to make love to her. He'd hesitated only because she'd caught him by surprise. God help him, it hadn't been because he hadn't wanted her. But she'd thought he was rejecting her, like her parents had rejected her. An odd pain had ripped through him then—he'd wanted to comfort her.

You've never been a substitute.

If he hadn't known better, he'd have thought she was telling the truth. There was no other man between them. Even now, she made him feel as if he was the only man who could do it for her, the only man to turn her on. Dammit, she'd even said so.

I want you, Tate.

Only you.

But was she just good at pretending? What was he to believe? *Who* was he to believe? The sexy woman who'd been in his arms back there, or the woman who knew how to wind him up like a watch? He had to find the truth, and the only way to do that was to open himself up a little and let her in. She'd either prove her worth…or reveal she was merely a fake.

Seven

When they arrived at his parents' place, Gemma was dismayed to find Tate's whole family there for the lunch. She'd expected his parents, perhaps his sister, but definitely not his grandmother. Helen still lived in her own home, so it made sense that Jonathan would invite his mother. Why Gemma hadn't expected her to be there today, she didn't know.

Of course, now she felt even more self-conscious about what had happened with Tate, as if the all-wise, elderly woman could actually see they had become lovers again. Considering they were married now, it would be a reasonable assumption to make anyway, but it made Gemma more than uncomfortable. What had happened between her and Tate was private.

"So what's happening about those pictures?" Tate's sister asked, before anyone had a chance to say more than a few words of greeting.

Tate's mouth tightened as he let his mother take Nathan from him. "I'm working on it."

"You realize what's out there in cyberspace stays out there forever, don't you?"

"Stop exaggerating, Bree," her father said from the bar in the corner, where he was pouring drinks.

Bree spun toward him. "I'm not exaggerating, Dad. Ask anyone."

"Give it a rest, sis," Tate growled, echoing Gemma's thoughts, and probably everyone else's, too. It seemed as if his sister was deliberately stirring up trouble.

Could Bree have been the one to take the pictures and put them on the internet?

"My, look at this little one," Darlene said in a calming voice as she sat down with her grandson on her lap. "He's such a little man now." It was clear she was trying to change the subject. "He looks like Gemma, but he reminds me of you at that age, Tate."

The words drew Tate's attention to his son, and his face relaxed. "Does he now?"

"Oh, yes. You were a beautiful little boy."

"Gee, thanks," Tate said. He gave her a crooked smile, but there was the usual hint of hardness as he looked at his mother. "Just what a grown man wants to hear."

Darlene's eyes flickered. "There's nothing wrong with a mother thinking her son is beautiful, no matter what his age." She sent her daughter-in-law an encouraging smile. "Isn't that right, Gemma?"

No matter what was going on between mother and son, at least Darlene wasn't holding anything against her. Gemma was grateful for the other woman's support. "I couldn't agree more, Darlene. Our sons will always be beautiful to us."

"Yeah, but thinking it and saying it out loud are two

different things," Tate drawled, giving Gemma a hooded look that made her acutely aware of everything that had happened between them back in their drawing room. His male possession had been totally consuming and irreversibly branding. At one time, she would have reveled in it. Right now all she wanted to do was get those perceptive eyes off her. Would he think she was putty in his hands now, not just physically but in every other way? No, that wouldn't happen. She wouldn't let it.

"Er…what was Tate like as a child?" she asked, dragging her gaze back to her mother-in-law.

Darlene beamed. "Oh, he was—"

"Best to ask Jonathan that question," Tate's grandmother interrupted her, speaking for the first time and not in a friendly tone. "I'd say he knows his son better than anyone."

The animation left Darlene's face and suddenly there was awkwardness in the air. It was as if Helen had been trying to make a point at her daughter-in-law's expense.

Then Jonathan came toward them carrying drinks. "No, I'll let Darlene answer that one, Mother." He smiled lovingly at his wife. "Go on, sweetheart."

Darlene looked at her husband, then nodded gratefully and put on a smile. "Now what was I saying? Oh, yes. Tate was a beautiful child with a sweet nature." She glanced at Bree. "So was my darling daughter," she added, and her eyes filled with motherly bemusement. "Of course, right from the start they both had their moments."

"We wouldn't be Chandlers if we didn't," Bree quipped, and everyone smiled.

Gemma looked at Tate, whose expression had closed up and who now had his hands thrust in his trouser pockets. She realized the awkwardness wasn't only between Helen and Darlene. The tension was between mother and son, a tension that Tate didn't have with his grandmother. The warm feeling between grandmother and grandson was obviously reciprocated. At the wedding, Helen had shown more than a soft spot for Tate. Hadn't the elderly woman hinted at being worried Gemma would hurt him? Helen couldn't be such an unfeeling person then.

So why pick on poor Darlene?

Gemma asked herself that question a couple more times during the delicious lunch as everything returned to normal and the only person Helen appeared to be slightly reserved with now was *her*.

Back to square one.

Or was it? All afternoon Tate watched her, stepping in and changing the subject, or getting her away from his grandmother whenever the woman focused on her in the smallest way. It was as if he was protecting her, now that he knew all she had suffered at the hands of her parents. Offering an olive branch? Okay, so it was more like a twig, but it didn't mean any less.

But on the way home it wasn't the tension between Tate and his family that worried her. It was the heightening awareness between the two of *them*—the feeling that after this morning, an arm's length wasn't enough.

Did she really want it to be?

"About my parents," she said, trying to get back to normalcy. "Thank you for sticking up for me. I really do appreciate it."

Tate gave her a pleased sideways glance. "You're welcome." Then, in an instant, there was something more in his look, as if he was remembering making love to her.

She dragged in a breath and searched for something else to say. "Doesn't your grandmother like your mother?"

Oh, dear.

His hands tightened on the wheel, but he kept his eyes on the road. "Why do you say that?"

She'd been trying to dispel the sexual tension inside the car. Instead, she'd replaced it with another type of tension.

She wrinkled her nose. "Just something in the air when they're in the same room."

"I hadn't noticed."

Her gut feeling said that wasn't the truth. Something was going on here. Yet was it really any of her concern? In spite of being grateful that he'd supported her today, she hadn't wanted him messing in her affairs before now. He wouldn't like her messing with his. She let it be.

It was a relief to arrive home and get out of the car. Inside the house, all was quiet.

Not for long, though, not with a one-year-old in the house. Nathan had been thoroughly spoiled all afternoon by the Chandlers, so it took a great deal of patience to get him through dinner, a bath and in his crib.

"Is he asleep?" Tate asked quietly behind her, making her jump as she backed out of Nathan's room.

She spun around. Tate was right there in front of her. Up close. "Almost."

"I thought I'd order pizza for dinner."

"P-pizza?"

"You used to love pizza."

"I still do." Her stomach fluttered. They had once shared a pizza and then made love. Of course, Tate had grown up wealthy, so delivered pizza had been a novelty for him. As *she* had no doubt been a novelty for him...

"I'll leave a note for Peggy that we don't want to be disturbed."

"Won't she—" She paused.

Amusement lit up his eyes. "What?"

She could feel herself blushing. "You know."

"Think I'm having my 'wicked way' with you?" His gaze roamed her face. "That's exactly what I intend to do. Again and again." Giving her the full force of his charisma, he lowered his head, his lips seeking hers…just as Nathan started to cry. Tate hovered above her mouth. "We could let him keep crying," he murmured.

She hardly dared move. "We could."

The crying got louder.

He inhaled deeply, straightened and gave a wry smile. "You'd better go see to our son." Before she could move away, he put his hand under her chin and kissed her quick. "Then later, lady, I intend to see to *you*. And I intend to take my time doing so."

Gemma had already pictured herself locked against his naked body, but his words reminded her of something she had to say. Nathan could wait a few moments more. His was a tired cry, not a hurting one.

She nervously wet her lips. "I know we didn't use… er…protection this morning, but I am on the pill now. I started taking it a few weeks ago when you said we were getting married. I just thought I'd say so. In case you were worried."

"I'm not." He raised an eyebrow but was watchful. "Are you?"

"No." Having his baby again and sharing in the wonder of it, knowing Tate would be pleased to be a part of it this time, would be wonderful. If only…no, she wouldn't wish for more. She didn't need more to give their children a happy life, she told herself.

He frowned. "There's a problem?"

She couldn't tell him her thoughts. "The doctor did say it may not be fully effective for another few weeks."

His face relaxed. "Then we'll take extra precautions in

future." He ran a finger along her chin. "And from now on we're sharing a bed."

"Are you sure?"

"There's no going back now."

She silently agreed. It would be too cruel to return to a platonic marriage. "No, there isn't."

His mistrust of her hadn't been resolved, but she had hopes they could move past it now that there was a renewed connection between them. Their married life had truly begun. And that was a scary but exhilarating thought.

By the time the pizzas arrived, Gemma had showered and changed into slacks and a knit top, and Nathan was asleep in his crib.

She and Tate ate opposite each other at the breakfast bar in the kitchen. There was no playfulness between them, but there was a definite heat that had been building all evening. This time was too serious, too important, to be messing around about it all. She didn't offer to hand-feed Tate any of her slice, and he didn't offer to lick her fingers clean, but oh, my, she could see he was thinking it, and remembering.

She had just finished washing down her second slice with a soda when she heard a rumble in Tate's chest. "Enough," he said in a strangled tone, dropping his pizza back in the box and surging to his feet. He came around the breakfast bar and pulled her to her feet. "Come on. We're going to bed."

Anticipation thumped inside her. "But I haven't finished," she said inanely.

"Neither have I." He didn't smile. He didn't stop. He led her out of the room and kept right on going until they were upstairs in his bedroom, where he quietly closed the door behind them and flicked on the light.

A hush fell.

His eyes took on an intensity that surprised her. "Now...what was that about taking our time..." He moved slowly closer, standing right in front of her, cupping her shoulders.

Time slowed.

Bending his head forward, he covered her mouth with his and kissed her gently. She'd expected a hungry kiss, but it was none the less potent for its gentleness. She closed her eyes and let herself feel him, feel the moment between them.

After a while he drew back. She missed his lips already and made a sound, but she forgave him when he brought her fingers to his lips. One by one, he kissed her fingertips, then the inside of her palm, next the tender skin of her wrist. He moved up her arm, to the curve of her shoulder.

"I remember that," he murmured, slipping his hand around her nape, looking into her eyes.

Her breath quivered. "What?"

"The little hitching sound you make in your throat when I touch you."

"I can't help it."

"I know." He dipped his lips to her throat, stealing her breath away.

Soon he leaned back and unhurriedly peeled off her clothes—her knit top, her bra...then her slacks and panties—exposing her until she was fully naked.

"Oh, yeah, I remember it all," he said huskily.

Sensations raced along her nerves, making her ache with wanting him. He stroked her breast then bowed his head to it. He circled her nipple with his tongue, then caught it between his lips and sucked.

She heard the hitch in her throat then.

And heard it again when he moved to her other breast.

His fingers started down her belly, heading for the apex of curls, and the hitch turned to a longing moan. She wanted him to touch her there. Oh, how she wanted him to touch her and touch her and keep right on touching her.

And then she wanted to touch *him*.

She put her hand against his chest and when she pushed him away she saw his surprise. "Let me." She brushed her lips over his as she pressed her palms against him, steadying herself and soaking up the feel of muscle beneath his shirt.

She undid his buttons slowly, starting at the lowest.

"You used to be much faster than this," he muttered in bemusement. "Not that I'm complaining."

"I was always in a hurry before." She'd been in love with him and she'd instinctively tried to grab all she could before it disappeared like the wind, which it had. Tonight she would take it slower and make memories. She would keep their future alive as long as possible.

Finally she undid the last button and slid his shirt off, loving the way his heartbeat thumped in his chest. She placed her lips to that beating heart and he groaned.

"You are a beautiful, beautiful man," she whispered. She moved her lips over his skin, swirling her tongue through the wisps of hair, the heat rising off him like a sultry day.

Her tongue prowled down toward his trousers.

All at once she was lifted, thrown over his shoulder. He carried her to the large bed, where he let her down on the duvet. She flopped back against it, her legs dangling over the edge, her naked body his to view.

She rose on her elbows, slightly embarrassed by the way she was positioned, slightly confused by the speed with which he'd changed everything. "I thought you said slow?"

"I didn't say torture," he muttered. He went down on his knees, parting her legs to lick through the dark vault already pre-moistened by her desire for him. She bucked at the touch of him. He began stroking his tongue up and down and soon put his hands on her hips to hold her still, allowing her to rise and fall but not escape. Not that she wanted to.

He tormented her with his mouth, and everything inside her grew to a fever pitch. She held his head to her, one minute gripping tight, then tunneling her fingers through his hair. He was touching the heart of her, and she couldn't hold back for much longer. He was rapidly bringing her to the edge of release, his tongue delightful and incredibly effective.

Then he buried his tongue deeper and she didn't have the slightest chance of staying in control. She willingly jumped into the most glorious oblivion.

By the time she had the strength to open her eyes, he had taken off his clothes and was sliding on a condom. She'd missed her opportunity to repay the favor, but he moved her backward on the bed so he could join their bodies. She didn't mind. She took him inside her, surrounding him, and knew this was just right, just how it should be between a man and a woman.

Excitement raced through her veins, followed by another tumult of emotions. Like a far-off light coming closer, they got brighter and brighter. Then it hit her: saying "Only you" was as close as she could get to saying "I love you."

Oh, God, she still loved him.

She'd never stopped loving him.

He was imprinted in her heart for always.

She looked into eyes that were dark in concentration. It

was Tate who made this special for her. *He* was the reason she was edging toward heaven, storming the gates, pushing them open.

She wanted to tell him.

Oh, Lord, she wanted to tell him.

But from somewhere deep inside, she drew on an inner strength she didn't know she had, somehow managing to hold back the words of love she knew could destroy her if she uttered them.

Yet she needed to say something.

"Only you, Tate," she cried out breathlessly as she felt herself being swallowed up by something bigger than the both of them.

And she knew then that no matter what had gone before, no matter what had been, this time in this man's arms she had truly come of age.

After they made love again, in the shower, Gemma lay in Tate's arms listening to his breathing, which was relaxed by sleep. The knowledge that she still loved him filled her with joy, and fear. There was so much more at stake this time. They'd found a profound togetherness when he was a part of her, but she knew it didn't extend beyond those bonded moments. Not for him anyway.

She wanted so much to tell him of her love, but how could she open herself to more hurt? He didn't love her, and he wouldn't hesitate to hurt her again if he thought she'd done the wrong thing again. She only had to remember how he'd reacted to finding her kissing his best friend. He'd been so angry he'd kicked her out of his life. Could it happen again? Drake was still around, wasn't he? And even if he wasn't, Tate still didn't fully trust her. The littlest thing could bring her world toppling down one more time.

Last time he'd kicked her out, she'd gone because she'd had to. Then she'd picked herself up because she'd had to. But if it happened again and she lost her son and her home and the man she loved all at once, she didn't think she'd recover. No organization, no book, no counseling, no amount of self-help would repair her broken heart. Her love for him would never die. It was inside her. It was a part of her. It was love at its powerful best, and that meant it had the capacity to do the most damage.

No, she wasn't willing to tell him.

Thankfully, right then, his mouth sought hers, and her thoughts were soon silenced by the man she loved.

Eight

"Peggy, I'd like you to move Gemma's things into my room today," Tate said at breakfast the next morning, making Gemma's heart jump.

The housekeeper wasn't quick enough to hide her surprise, though Tate's note about not wanting to be disturbed last night must have given her a clue that this would happen. A moment later, Peggy smiled at them both with clear pleasure. "I'd be happy to, Mr. Chandler."

Somehow Gemma managed not to blush, even as she remembered Tate having his "wicked way" with her last night. Three times in fact—three times where she'd had to work hard at not giving herself away—reminding herself that her love for him was a secret. It was a matter of self-preservation.

"We'll do it together, Peggy," Gemma said, thinking she could make a game of it with Nathan while Tate was at the office.

Her heart was light as she and Peggy moved her things into the other suite. With two walk-in closets, there was no need to move any of Tate's stuff to make room for hers. Of course, she couldn't help but think that her clothes from before her marriage wouldn't have taken up a quarter of this space. And it would have only taken a minute to move them.

She kept an eye on Nathan in his playpen as she and Peggy moved back and forth with the expensive dresses, slacks and blouses, coats, swimsuits, everything for any occasion, including her underwear. She blushed at the memory of Tate stripping the scraps of material from her body with total precision.

"I'll just pop downstairs and get some more drawer liners," Peggy said a short while later. "This closet has never been used, and those are looking a bit faded."

Gemma was pleased that no other woman had shared this suite, this house, with Tate. "Take your time, Peggy," she said, flopping down on the bed and taking a breather.

The housekeeper left the room and was heading down the stairs when the telephone rang. Gemma was closest to the phone, so she called out that she'd get it.

She soon wished she hadn't.

"Hello, Gemma."

Drake!

She stood up. "Tate's at the office, as you must know."

"How would I know that? I thought he and you might still be on your honeymoon."

"You could have called him on his cell phone to find out."

"Then I'd miss talking to you, wouldn't I?"

"Drake, stop it."

He sighed as if she were being unreasonable. "Gemma,

you're my best friend's wife now. I'm merely attempting to make amends."

She'd never believe that.

"Anyway," he continued, "I was phoning to commiserate with Tate about those nasty pictures of your old apartment going around the internet. I thought he might be upset about them."

Her heart lurched inside her chest. "How do you know about them?"

"I was talking to Bree earlier."

More and more, Gemma believed Bree was the one behind all this. "She had no right telling you anything."

"I'm Tate's best friend. She thought I might be able to help in some way."

Or cause trouble.

"You know, Gemma, it's never wise to be complacent about these things."

It was a warning that she shouldn't be complacent about her marriage. Suddenly it hit her. Bree wasn't behind those pictures at all.

It was Drake.

"I could say the same to you," she said, trying to keep her voice from shaking. He wanted to hear how he was getting to her.

"Gem, I don't know what you mean. I'm merely trying to be a friend to you both."

God, she hated him calling her "Gem," hated the smugness in his voice. "You were never a friend of mine, Drake. Or of Tate's, if he only but knew it. One day he'll see you for what you are."

"There's nothing to see."

Gemma opened her mouth to spout something scathing, but she heard a noise in the doorway and her head snapped up to see Peggy standing there. "Er…I have to go now.

Please call Tate on his cell phone if you need to talk to him." She hung up and fought to keep her face blank.

A moment crept by.

Peggy frowned. "Mrs. Chandler, I hope you don't think I'm being forward, but if you need to talk—"

Gemma tried to look casual. "Thank you, Peggy, but I'm fine." She was tempted to ask what the other woman had heard, but she was sure Tate wouldn't appreciate her discussing their marriage with anyone, much less their employee. Besides, she didn't want Peggy thinking she had heard anything of importance.

"I thought you might need a friend."

"Thank you." Gemma gave a half-hearted smile. "I can always do with more friends."

Peggy didn't look convinced, but she was professional enough to leave things be. Gemma took advantage of that and remained close-lipped about it all, acting as if nothing out of the ordinary had happened.

Still, she was relieved once they'd finished moving and Peggy had gone back downstairs. With Nathan taking a small nap, she had some time to think about things away from prying eyes. She couldn't contemplate the phone call before now, in case Peggy read her face and related her worries to Tate. As it was, Gemma hoped Peggy would keep her own counsel.

Damn Drake for this. He knew he had her running scared and that she wouldn't say anything to Tate. If only Tate had heard the conversation, then he'd believe her. Perhaps she could record Drake's call next time, she thought with a flash of hope.

On second thought, there wasn't any guarantee that Tate or anyone else would hear the same smugness that she'd heard. She wasn't imagining it, but Tate might not believe that.

God, this was like navigating around quicksand, in the dark, with Drake hot on her tail. She dare not even reach out a hand to Tate and ask him to help her. If she did, she might find the man she loved wasn't prepared to save her while sacrificing his best friend.

Not even for Nathan's sake.

Mid-afternoon, Gemma took Nathan to the kitchen for a snack and found Peggy at the island, chopping food. With thoughts of Drake filling her mind, and on edge about all he was capable of doing to her marriage, Gemma hesitated in the doorway. She was still afraid that the housekeeper might say something to Tate, however inadvertently.

Peggy looked up and blinked. "Oh, Gemma, you startled me. I was miles away."

Gemma put aside her worries. "Sorry." She stepped into the room with Nathan on her hip. "What are you making?"

"Apple pie for tonight's dessert."

"Homemade? Yum. I love apple pie. My mother used to make them," she said, not thinking. Her heart wrenched at the reminder of her parents and yesterday's events. She tried to ignore it. "Can I help?"

Peggy must have seen something on her face. The housekeeper wouldn't know about yesterday's visit, but she would certainly remember her parents hadn't been at the wedding. A touch of concern filled the older woman's eyes and she gave a kind smile. "Why not?" She held up a slice of apple. "Would Nathan like a piece?"

"Sure."

Gemma strapped Nathan in his high chair and gave him the apple, and soon she was busy slicing and rolling out the pastry. The fruit cooked on the stove, the sweet smell of apple and cinnamon wafting in the air. They had an enjoyable time and ended up making two thick, delicious-looking apple pies.

"We'll never eat all this," Gemma said ruefully as they surveyed their handiwork.

"You don't know my Clive. He'd eat a full one himself."

As Tate walked into the kitchen, the sound of Gemma's soft chuckle sent his pulse hammering. She stood with her hands on her slim hips, her blond hair slightly mussed, her gorgeous mouth curved in a smile. She was certainly a picture to come home to. In fact, the whole scene made him feel good about his life. A beautiful wife, a handsome son and a motherly housekeeper who had adopted them as if they were her own.

A sense of satisfaction filled him. This was his family. He'd been sitting at his desk and hadn't wanted to work. He'd wanted to see Gemma and Nathan. He'd actually missed them. It was a strangely powerful feeling that, surprisingly, gave him more pleasure than the corporate world he loved so much. He hadn't realized what had been missing from his life before this.

Gemma suddenly saw him, and panic flared in her eyes. "Tate! You're home early."

He scanned her face. Did she expect him to be the bearer of bad news? He supposed he couldn't blame her for jumping to conclusions. It always seemed to be bad news for her lately.

"I thought we might take Nathan for an ice cream and a walk to the park," he said, putting her mind at rest. He glanced at his son in his high chair. "But he looks pretty happy here with the measuring cups."

Her whole body visibly relaxed. "Oh, yes, that would be lovely."

"It's a glorious day outside," Peggy said encouragingly.

Just then, Nathan let out a wail. There was a small red mark on his forehead where he'd obviously hit himself. Gemma swung their son up in her arms, cuddling him until the crying subsided.

"Is he okay?" Tate asked, an odd feeling in his chest as he watched her mothering his child.

"Yes, he's fine." She rechecked the fading mark on Nathan's forehead, then smiled at the adults. "But I'm sure an ice cream will make it much better."

Peggy laughed. "I'm sure it will."

Tate remembered how he'd been looking forward to taking them to the park. "I'll just go change out of this suit." He glanced at Gemma. "When can you be ready?"

Gemma looked at Peggy. "Do you need any more help?"

The housekeeper shooed her on. "No, we're finished here. I'll clean up."

"Thanks, Peggy. I had fun."

"Me, too, Gemma." Peggy darted a guilty look at Tate, before spinning away toward the sink. He was tempted to invite her to call him by his name again but it would be a waste of breath. Neither she nor Clive would budge on this.

"I'll come upstairs with you and change Nathan's diaper before we go," Gemma said.

Tate waited for her in the doorway. "Let me carry him. He's heavy." He lifted Nathan out of her arms and they left the kitchen. "I'm still amazed at your accomplishment," he said, as they headed for the stairs.

One finely shaped eyebrow rose. "What accomplishment?"

"Getting Peggy to call you Gemma." He grimaced

ruefully as they stopped at Nathan's room. "She still calls me Mr. Chandler."

Gemma flashed him a smile. "We women have our ways."

His eyes dropped to that mouth. "That you do."

Gemma's cheeks held a soft blush. Her reaction filled him with pleasure and stirred his blood.

"You've got flour on your ear." He reached out and ran the pad of his thumb over her earlobe, making her jump. "By the way, I'd ask you to join me in the shower but—"

Her blush deepened. "Don't say that in front of Nathan."

He was amused. "He doesn't understand what I'm saying."

"I know, but—"

He took pity on her and cut her off with a quick kiss. "Go change him."

They would have tonight.

The walk to the park was companionable and leisurely. They enjoyed sitting on the bench and eating their ice creams. There was no sight of the children and the puppy from the other week, but the playground was busy with kids ridding themselves of energy built up in the classroom.

Tate realized Gemma was staring off into space, chewing her lip. "You seem distracted."

She blinked. "Do I? Sorry, I was just thinking about something." She turned away to drop Nathan's now-empty ice cream cup in the bin nearest her.

Tate didn't know why, but Drake slashed through his mind. The thought turned his blood cold, making him glad of his dark sunglasses.

Yet for once he pushed thoughts of Drake aside, not wanting to jump to conclusions. He didn't want the other man spoiling this moment between him and his family.

She attempted a smile. "It's good to get out like this, don't you think?"

"Yes."

She picked up after that, but during the evening, as they ate dinner, then watched a movie together before making love, he couldn't shake the feeling that something still wasn't right. She was pretending it was, but it wasn't.

It could be about her parents, he told himself as he lay in bed in the dark with Gemma asleep in his arms. It was only yesterday they'd been here causing havoc and heartache for their daughter. God, they had a lot to answer for.

And then another thought hit him.

Perhaps *he* had a lot to answer for, too.

As quickly as it had come, he dismissed that thought, not liking the guilt that rose inside him. He'd had a right to be angry about Drake, and a right to be angry about Gemma not telling him about Nathan. Just because he felt sorry for her now didn't mean *he* was at fault.

Even though it felt like he was.

Nine

So many times over the following week, Gemma wished she could tell Tate she believed Drake had posted the pictures of her apartment. But despite her husband making love to her every day, despite him coming home early on a regular basis, she was very much aware of how fragile their marriage was.

Then, at the end of that week, Tate finally volunteered the information that every trail seemed to lead to a dead end, though the investigator hadn't given up. She could have pointed him in the right direction, of course, but at what cost? At least Drake had not called back.

Thankfully, her marriage had slipped out of the media's radar for the moment, and with the awards dinner only a few days away, she began to relax. Time would dull the pain of Tate thinking she'd kissed Drake, and the pain of Tate not believing her denial. She wished she could talk to him about Drake as easily as she'd talked to him about her parents. How she wished he would be equally as understanding. Unfortunately, she knew that wouldn't happen.

And then…life rolled onto the next crisis.

One evening after Nathan was in bed, Tate flicked through the television channels. Out of the blue, an older couple appeared on the screen.

"What the hell!" Tate exclaimed, sitting forward.

Gemma's heart rose in her chest. "Th-that's my parents!"

He darted a look at Gemma. "I'll turn it off. You don't need to hear this." He went to press the remote button.

"No!" She swallowed. "Leave it on."

He paused. "Are you sure?"

She nodded, her eyes already returning to her parents' interview on one of those current affairs programs. To say she felt betrayed was an understatement. She felt like she'd been speared right through the heart.

It only got worse. They talked about being unable to control her as a teenager, about how she'd left home too young, breaking their hearts. How they'd let her come back home, single and pregnant, but she'd walked out again.

"That's not true," she whispered in disbelief, trying to accept that they could hurt her even more than they already had. "They've twisted it all around." She'd left home at twenty because of them. And they'd *asked* her to leave when they learned she was pregnant.

"It's a sob story, that's all," Tate growled.

And everyone would believe it.

Then they said how they hadn't been invited to their own daughter's wedding, and when they'd come to see Gemma and their grandson, they'd been asked to leave.

"But they didn't even ask to see Nathan," she cried.

Tate's eyes were hard. "I was there, Gemma. I saw what they were like."

"I never thought they'd do something like this. I know they had to save face, but this—"

"You're being too generous, as usual."

Her mind swirled with confusion. "Why now? It's been nearly two weeks since we saw them."

"My guess is it's about the awards dinner on Friday. They're probably trying to put a stop to my family getting the award because they're jealous that you and Nathan are Chandlers now."

"But they didn't want me...or Nathan," she choked, jumping to her feet, trying to shake off the anguish.

Tate stood up and pulled her into his arms. "I know, sweetheart."

She buried her face against his chest, the endearment warming her before another thought kicked in. She jerked her head back to look up at him. "Your family won't be happy about this, Tate."

He didn't hesitate. "They won't hold this against you." His jaw clenched as he looked past her to the television. "Your family will be retracting this, I promise."

"But it'll be too late for the award. They've already done a lot of damage."

"No, they're wrong. It's related to the award but it won't affect it at all. If the board was going to withdraw the honor, they would have done it before now."

She supposed that was true. Part of the reason they'd married in a hurry was to protect the family name.

He put one hand under her chin. "You'd better stay home tomorrow. And don't answer the telephone. I'll beef up security."

She hadn't planned on anything but a lovely, relaxing

day with her son, but now… "They're not nice people, are they?" she said on a ragged breath.

Tate gave her a soft kiss. "No, they're not. And you're not like them at all," he said, meaning it.

Gemma didn't sleep well, and she knew Tate hadn't either. He offered to stay home with her the next morning, but she thanked him and told him no. She was in danger of throwing herself a "pity party," and she needed to do it alone.

Of course, once their son was up and about, Nathan's smiling face put things into perspective. How could she mope about when she could be with her child? Every moment with him was precious.

As was every moment with Tate, she thought, as he kissed her goodbye on his way to the office. And a tender kiss it was, too. Loving him might be one-sided, but having this man in her life was more important than anything her family could do to her.

Her head was in a better place, but she was still startled when Peggy showed her mother-in-law into the sunroom just after lunch. Had Darlene been sent to find out more about Gemma's parents? Or was she here to take Gemma to task for bringing further disrepute on the Chandler name?

Gemma gestured for Darlene to sit on the sofa, then she sat, too. "It's nice to see you, Darlene," she said warily, once Peggy went off to get them refreshments.

"It's always lovely to see you, Gemma, but I thought you might need my support today."

Gemma's heart warmed. "That's very sweet of you."

Darlene looked around the bright and airy sunroom. "Where's my grandson? Asleep?"

"Yes, I'm trying to get him to nap after lunch instead of in the late morning."

As if by silent agreement, they spoke about general things until Peggy brought refreshments and left them to it.

"Tate dropped by the house this morning to explain about your parents," Darlene said, once they were alone again. Sympathy filled her expression. "I can't believe what they did to you, not just now, but in the past. It must have been devastating when they turned their backs on you."

Gemma swallowed. Her mother-in-law was a kind person, but Gemma hadn't expected actual compassion. "It was," she murmured with a catch in her throat. Then, in case Darlene couldn't say what she might need to say, Gemma took the bull by the horns. "I'm really sorry to bring your family into this."

"We're your family now, too, you know."

Gemma blinked. She wanted to cry in gratitude. "Thank you. That means a lot to me." She released a shuddering breath. "Being a part of a family again is wonderful, and being a part of your family is terrific." She wouldn't mention that she hadn't felt quite at home with the other Chandlers.

There was a short silence as Darlene nodded. "I know they're not perfect but..." Without warning, her mother-in-law burst into tears.

Gemma stared for a moment. "Darlene?"

Darlene tried to speak but cried even harder as she grabbed for a hankie from her handbag. Gemma could only watch with concern until the woman got herself partly under control.

"Forgive me, Gemma," Darlene sniffed. "I didn't come here to talk about my problems."

Her mother-in-law had problems? "If you want to talk,

I'm here to listen. And I promise I won't say anything to anyone. You can trust me."

The older woman looked at her. "Yes, I think I can. I haven't known you very long, but I feel close to you, Gemma." She paused. "I'm talking about your parents but…" She gave a small sob. "I've not been such a good parent myself. You see…" Sob. "I had an affair years ago."

Shock rolled through Gemma. "*You* had an affair?"

"Yes. And please don't think too badly of me," she said quickly.

"Of course not. I'm just really…surprised. You and Jonathan have such a great marriage."

Darlene nodded and wiped her wet cheeks. "We do now. We didn't then." She winced. "You see, Jonathan was never one to show his feelings. I hope I don't embarrass you by saying this. He's a passionate man in the bedroom, but not even after we were married did he once tell me he loved me." She took a shaky breath. "Oh, I knew he did, but it's not the same as hearing the words."

Gemma understood only too well.

Darlene's eyes started to fill with tears again, but she rapidly blinked them back. "We'd been married about fifteen years when I finally realized I would never hear those words from Jonathan. He was working hard and it seemed he needed me less and less. I was starting to feel not only like less of a woman but like less of a wife."

Gemma reached out and patted the other woman's hand. "That's understandable."

She took a breath. "And then one day I met this man. I was shopping in one of the department stores. I dropped my bag and he picked it up and we sort of clicked. He asked me to have a coffee with him. I knew I shouldn't, but I was feeling low. Jonathan hadn't made love to me for months. Just the night before I'd tried to make the first move in bed, and he'd said he was too tired."

"Was Jonathan having an affair?"

"Oh, no, that wasn't the problem. He was just so focused on work and making money. He had some pretty big shoes to fill. His father was such a force, you see." She gave a quiet sigh. "Anyway, this man and I started to meet for coffee. His marriage wasn't very good either. I was still desperate to get Jonathan's attention, but one thing led to another and I decided I was in love with the other man. I couldn't take my marriage anymore, so I packed my things and left."

Gemma's eyes widened. "You *left?*"

"Yes. I planned on going for good. I told myself the children didn't really need me and were probably better off without me in their lives. I knew Helen would step into the breach, you see. Of course, I was just making excuses for myself." There was a tiny pause. "I was back a week later."

"Only a week?"

She nodded. "Jonathan was shattered, and he begged me to come home. By that time, I realized I'd made a mistake. I regret what I did, but it's been the making of our marriage. It seemed to open up something inside him, and he's been a loving husband and father ever since."

"How old were Tate and Bree?"

Her face crumpled again. "Tate was twelve and Bree seven. Oh, God, I felt so terrible about that." She stopped and took a moment to control herself, then she managed to speak further. "Bree was too young, but Tate knew. He was colder to me when I came back, and he's been reserved with me ever since." Deep regret was etched in her face. "I couldn't bring myself to explain it to my son. Sometimes I wish I had."

Gemma's heart squeezed for the young teenage boy whose world had turned upside down. Suddenly, she realized this explained why Tate had reacted so strongly when he thought *she* was cheating with Drake. After all, they'd only been together a month when that accidental kiss between her and his best friend had happened. Another man would probably have brushed her off like a fly and never looked back. Tate had held a grudge because of the memories of his mother betraying his father. She certainly didn't think now that it was because *she* personally had hurt him. It wasn't possible to hurt someone if there was no true emotional involvement between them.

"Unfortunately," Darlene continued, bringing Gemma back to the discussion, "Helen and Nathaniel never forgave me."

And that explained the coolness Helen showed for her daughter-in-law, a coolness that had been extended to *her* because the matriarch thought Gemma had done wrong by her grandson.

And yet... "Maybe I should keep quiet about this, but shouldn't Helen and Nathaniel have taken some responsibility for putting such pressure on Jonathan in the first place?"

Darlene looked surprised, then gratified. "I've always thought so, too." She sighed. "It's too late now. Nothing's ever going to change with my mother-in-law. I hurt her son, and that's all that matters to her."

"It's a pity you never had it out with her," Gemma said, thinking out loud.

"Oh, I couldn't." She seemed to catch herself. "Could I?"

Gemma hadn't meant to get involved at all, but it wouldn't hurt to support Darlene. Her mother-in-law had supported her in everything so far. "You don't have anything to lose now by talking to Helen, do you? Your marriage to Jonathan is rock solid."

"Yes, it is. And it *is* time to clear the air. She's always been snippy with me in private, but lately..." A determined look crossed Darlene's face. She rose from the sofa. "Thank you, Gemma. I'm going to do it right now."

Gemma got to her feet, suddenly not sure she should have encouraged the other woman. Perhaps she should have let things lie.

Yet the comment about Helen no longer keeping her animosity private worried her. Was Helen becoming bolder because Gemma had joined the family? Did the elderly lady feel she could now openly attack the two women who were "outsiders?" How far would this go? Perhaps it *was* time someone stood up to Helen, before things got worse.

"I guess you need to do what you need to do, Darlene. If I can help in any way, please let me know."

Darlene kissed her cheek. "I will. Thank you." She smiled. "I'm really pleased you don't have to go through all this with Tate. He's so caring and concerned about you. Jonathan was never like that with me."

Gemma was glad the other woman turned to pick up her handbag from the sofa right then and didn't see her reaction. Caring and concerned? Gemma supposed that was true. But Tate didn't love her. It made her wonder if the same thing might happen to them that had happened to his parents. If Tate's care and concern lessened over the next fifteen years, would *she* be tempted to take a lover? She didn't think so. She couldn't imagine ever wanting to be in anyone's arms but his. He was the only man she wanted.

The only man she'd ever wanted.

* * *

Gemma waited until Nathan was in bed before speaking to Tate about Darlene. She'd spent all afternoon thinking about his mother's visit and had decided she couldn't bear having the same thing happen to her marriage that had happened to her in-laws. The only way to prevent such a thing was to bring his mother's affair out in the open. But she was acutely aware that she needed to tread warily.

When they were sitting on the terrace having an after-dinner drink, watching the sun lower on the horizon, she said, "Your mother came to see me today."

Tate's brow lifted. "Did she?"

"She wanted to make sure I was okay."

"Good." He looked pleased. "I know she was concerned about you."

"She's a very caring person, isn't she?"

His eyes turned inscrutable as he paused to take a sip of his drink. "Yes."

Short.

Abrupt.

She took a deep breath, then, "She told me about her affair all those years ago."

He bolted upright, almost spilling his drink. "Jesus!"

She forged onward. "I understand where you're coming from now, Tate."

There was a flicker of raw emotion in his eyes. "If you breathe a word of this, I swear—"

Her eyes widened. "How could you think I would say anything to anyone? I wouldn't repay your mother that way."

"Damn it all," he muttered, setting his glass down on the table.

"You've never forgiven her, have you?"

The rawness in his eyes was replaced by a glower.

"That's none of your bloody business." He pushed to his feet.

"It is when you're making *me* pay for her mistake."

He stared down at her. "Did you tell her about us?"

"Of course not!" She was glad she hadn't mentioned Darlene's coming confrontation with Helen. She wouldn't give him any more ammunition to use against her.

He raised an eyebrow, cooler now and in control again. "Why so affronted? You can't deny you and my mother have a lot in common."

Her chin lifted a notch at his tone. It hadn't taken him long to return to his arrogant self. "I was never unfaithful to you, Tate."

"That's only in the truest sense, since we weren't married at the time. You can still be unfaithful in a moral sense." His mouth tightened. "And you were."

"A kiss is not the same as having sex," she snapped, then she could have bit out her tongue. He thought she had admitted to wanting Drake.

"It was two-timing, Gemma. Make no mistake about that."

Her gaze sharpened as she got up from the chair. "You always were quick to believe the worst of me. Now I'm wondering if you'd decided my time was up. You wanted to be rid of me, and believing Drake's lie was the easiest way to go about it."

He flinched. "That's bloody ridiculous."

"Is it? I'm not so sure."

"I caught you kissing him, dammit."

"I thought I was kissing *you*," she said, not for the first time and probably not the last.

He made a dismissive gesture. "I'm not going over this again, Gemma. Just know this. If I ever catch you kissing

Drake—or any other man for that matter—I'll take Nathan from you so fast your head will spin."

Underneath she shook, but Darlene's revelation allowed her to see beyond this old argument. For the first time, she could see the hurt beneath his stance. A hurt he masked with pure anger.

And with her understanding came a new outlook on how to manage him. "Then I have nothing to worry about," she said quietly and confidently. "I don't intend to kiss any other man except you."

As if bowled over by the statement, he stared at her for a long moment as if searching for the truth. Then his face underwent a subtle change, and she knew he believed she meant it. He gave an almost imperceptible nod before twisting on his heels and heading back inside through the patio doors.

She heard him leave the house soon after, and only then did she let herself slump down on the chair and think about what had just passed between them. In one way, it hadn't gone well. In another, it was a complete eye-opener.

Tate Chandler needed as much reassurance in his life as the next person—even if he would never acknowledge it.

Tate returned home late that evening. He'd spent a few hours at the office trying to work but hadn't succeeded. He'd been unable to concentrate after Gemma challenged him and his beliefs.

Had he forgiven his mother? she'd asked.

Short answer, no.

So he was blaming Gemma for his mother's mistake?

Gemma had made a mistake on her own. He didn't need his mother as an excuse.

He was quick to believe the worst, she'd said.

He'd seen what he'd seen.

He'd wanted a reason to end their relationship.

Actually, he'd felt more for her back then than for any other woman he'd ever known. Why he would want to—

Stop.

Rephrase.

His feelings hadn't come into it at all. He'd *wanted* Gemma more than he'd wanted any other woman, that's all. The reason he'd ended their affair was because he'd caught her kissing Drake. She'd betrayed his trust. She was grasping at straws by bringing his mother into it.

So why the hell had he believed her when she'd said she didn't intend to kiss any man but him? It was incredible that he could accept her statement as truth.

And yet, he did.

One thing was apparent. Over the past few weeks he'd seen a side of Gemma that went beyond sex. He'd seen her as a loving mother, a hurt and betrayed daughter. She was kind to everyone whether they were employees or people at the park. She cared about a teenager's personal problems, even though she had enough problems of her own. She was charming and beautiful, and she found his antics with his son amusing. She was someone he wanted to *be* with, in and out of the bedroom. That was quite an admission. For the first time, he felt hope that maybe their marriage might have a chance.

He had a lot to think about, was even now still thinking about it, as he came out of the shower and slipped into bed beside his wife. He pulled her against him so she could pillow her cheek on his chest. She fit so right against him.

Then, out of the blue, she half twisted on top of him, sliding one leg across his thighs as she stretched up to kiss him. He took the kiss, reveling in the feel of her against his thighs, but he could tell she was trying to tell him something.

He broke away from her mouth. "Gemma?"

"I'm here, Tate." She leaned her palms on his chest, deepened the kiss and adjusted her body, making him growl in his throat. She slid her hand down to where he was hard for her. "And I'm not going anywhere…"

She kissed the length of his throat, down the center of his chest. By the time she'd finished with him, they were both satisfyingly exhausted.

And he knew what she'd been trying to say.

She was staying with him, and nothing would stop her.

Ten

By the time the awards dinner rolled around on Friday night, Gemma was pinching herself. Something had changed between her and Tate. Something subtle but good. It was almost as if he actually trusted her.

Of course, he was still convinced she'd wanted Drake two years ago, and that continued to hurt her, but at least he seemed prepared to put it behind them.

She was praying Drake didn't turn up tonight to spoil things. After a while there didn't appear to be any empty chairs at their table, or any of the other tables. Once the room was full, she finally let out a slow sigh of relief.

Able to relax now, she noticed that Darlene and Helen seemed to be getting on well together and were talking like old friends. Thank heavens that had worked out. She'd worried she might have caused more friction between them. If Tate had found out, it might have damaged the thin trust between them.

"Did you have something to do with this?" Tate murmured in her ear, making her realize he'd been watching his mother and grandmother with a slightly confused look.

Gemma lifted a slim shoulder and shrugged. "I merely listened." And really, that's all she'd done.

An odd gratitude flared in his eyes, and she wondered if he was starting to look at his mother in a more forgiving light. There was a ways to go, but still…

"Thank you, Gemma." He kissed her softly on the lips.

The kiss took her by surprise, and love for him filled her up and threatened to overflow. Dare she believe his affection was developing into something more?

When she looked again, the others were smiling at her. Darlene and Jonathan looked pleased by the kiss, and Helen looked thoroughly delighted. Only Bree seemed puzzled, as well she should. Things in the Chandler family had changed for the better, but Tate's sister hadn't been told anything yet.

Gemma herself had been surprised by the warmth Tate's grandmother had shown her on arrival tonight. At first, she'd thought it was for show, but as Helen had spoken to her as if she was actually welcome in this family, she knew the elder woman had changed her tune. Thankfully, the others appeared to be following her lead.

Just then, the awards presentation commenced and there were speeches about the good things the Chandler family had done over the years. Finally, Helen was asked to center stage, and Jonathan walked his mother through a standing ovation.

The older woman waited until everyone was seated before speaking. "It's a great honor for me to be standing here tonight, accepting this award. As you know, my dear husband, Nathaniel, passed away only a couple of months ago, but he would have been thrilled to know…"

Gemma listened with a light heart. The Chandler family really did deserve this award, and she was so glad that nothing had stopped them from receiving it. She would never have been able to forgive herself if the award had been taken from them because of her actions…or because of her family's actions.

"And Nathaniel was all about family," Helen was saying, bringing Gemma back to the speech. "It's something my son has continued, and now, I'm pleased to say, my grandson, as well. As many of you know, Tate recently married, and his new wife and son have brought great joy to this family."

Gemma's heart lifted in surprise. How lovely of Helen to…

"Gemma is proving herself to be a valued member of our family. She joins my daughter-in-law, Darlene, and my granddaughter, Bree, in being women determined to make life better for their loved ones. Gemma had no decent example to follow growing up, so it's a measure of her as a person that she's so giving and strong."

Gemma sat there stunned, only vaguely aware of Tate picking up her hand and squeezing it. Helen was supporting her in public? She was telling everyone that Gemma's parents were in the wrong? Telling everyone not to believe what was on the internet or the television? Gemma hadn't expected such wholehearted support.

"And then there's my great-grandson," Helen continued. "Nathan joins us as the littlest member of my family, but certainly not the smallest in value."

Gemma was still trying to take it all in.

"Nathaniel would have been so proud to receive this

award for his family. I can see him sitting up in heaven, smiling down at us tonight. God bless."

The sound of applause was almost deafening. Jonathan escorted Helen back to the table, but before she sat down she kissed Gemma on the cheek in a display of public affection. The cameras clicked like wild things. Tears pooled in Gemma's eyes. This meant so much to her. Helen wasn't just being nice for the sake of the media. She was just being sincere.

All at once, Gemma needed some time to herself. "Excuse me for a minute." She got to her feet and grabbed her purse.

Tate put his hand on her arm. "Are you okay?"

She blinked back the tears and gave him a small smile. "Yes." But in case he thought she wasn't, she added, "Yes, I really am fine…now."

He smiled in understanding, and with that smile in her heart she hurried off to find the ladies' room. She didn't stop to talk to anyone as she weaved her way through the maze of tables, her eyes still watery from emotion.

It was a relief to get outside the ballroom. She tottered after a couple of women ahead of her down one of the corridors, figuring they were probably going to powder their noses. She couldn't help but marvel how things had turned around. It was a miracle come true. Tate's family had forgiven her. Now all she needed was for Tate to do the same.

Someone stepped in front of her and put his hands on her arms, forcing her to stop. "Hello, Gemma."

For a moment, Gemma didn't recognize the man in the dark dinner suit. Then her mind screeched to a stop. "Drake!"

"You sound surprised to see me."

She flinched and tried to draw back, but his hands

tightened on her upper arms. "Let me go," she said anxiously. She wanted to sound firm, but her emotions were high and the words came out like a plea.

Satisfaction entered his eyes. "Is that any way to treat an old friend?"

A flashback rolled over her. Dear God, if Tate saw them like this... "Drake, look—"

"I'm looking, sweetheart."

She found the strength to lift her hands to his chest, intending to push him away. "Please leave me alo—"

"Gemma?"

Oh, God.

The sound came from behind her and she twisted around to see Tate standing a few feet from them. The look in his eyes said it all. She could see his trust in her shriveling up, like a flash fire of betrayal had swept over him. He was disbelieving, angry, hurt... It was written on his face.

Gemma couldn't take any more. She'd lost Tate. Lost the man she loved. Again. All that was between them was no more.

And this time she would lose her son, too.

She felt herself slipping down to the carpet.

Tate stood for a moment in a no-man's-land, unable to move as his wife fainted in front of him. He felt sick to the stomach. He'd caught them again. They must have arranged to meet here, however briefly. They probably thought it was safer to meet in public.

Then something strange happened. He caught a glimpse of satisfaction on Drake's face. Suddenly, Tate wasn't sure about anything. He hadn't heard from Drake since before the wedding, and he hadn't contacted him about tonight either. He'd even felt guilty about it.

And Gemma needed him.

He started forward as an odd emotion rose up inside him like bile. She was *his* wife. No other man should be touching her. If Drake truly cared for Gemma, he'd already be on his knees beside her.

Hell, someone who truly cared wouldn't have let her hit the ground. Tate jumped the distance between them, pleased to see her eyes open as she tried to sit up. It was as well that Drake moved out of the way or Tate might have knocked the other man's head off for letting her fall.

"Gemma?" He half sat her against his body, allowing her to lean against him.

"I'm okay."

Looking down at her face, he saw the color coming back into her cheeks, though not in a good way. "You need a doctor."

She tried to get to her feet, but she looked agitated. "I'm fine."

Tate's arm tightened around her shoulders. "No, stay here for a moment."

"I'm sorry, man," Drake said quickly. "I didn't mean to run into Gemma like this."

Gemma's whole body tensed, and, for the first time, Drake's words didn't ring true to Tate. They matched the satisfaction he'd glimpsed on his best friend's face just moments before.

Yet he didn't want Drake to know even a hint of what he was thinking. He struggled to get his emotions under control. By the time he looked up, he knew no one would guess what was going through his mind. "I can handle it from here."

"Is there anything I can do?" Drake asked.

Tate felt a shiver run through Gemma. It wasn't about her wanting the other man. It was the opposite, in fact.

"Can you tell my family what's happened? They're in the ballroom." That at least would get Drake out of the way. "I'll call Clive to come collect us so I can take Gemma home."

"Sure. I'll go tell them right now. No need for you to worry." Drake walked away.

Tate followed him with his eyes. There was a definite swagger to his friend's back that sent a chill through him.

"Tate, it's not what you think."

He looked down at Gemma's anxious face and could see she thought he was upset with her. Hell, he couldn't be sure he *wasn't* upset with her. Deep down he was definitely upset with *someone*.

Then she flinched and something punched him in the chest. She looked like an injured animal expecting to be hurt. Had Drake done this to her?

Or had *he?*

"Come on," he said, helping her to her feet. "We'll go find somewhere for you to sit down until Clive gets here."

A couple of women came upon them and offered assistance. Tate didn't like others seeing this, but they were in a public place and it couldn't be helped. He took up their offer to show him and Gemma to a small sitting area down the next corridor. Once satisfied they were no longer needed, they went back to the ballroom.

Tate called Clive on his cell phone, explained the situation and was thankful the older man was only about five minutes away from the hotel. Clive usually liked to arrive early and chat with some of the other drivers.

The next minute, Bree came racing toward them. "What happened? Drake said Gemma fainted."

"She did, but she's okay now."

"Oh, good," Bree said, looking relieved.

Tate had to admit he was surprised by the concern on his sister's face. She hadn't exactly been friendly toward Gemma these past few weeks.

"It was probably too much excitement tonight," he excused, keeping Drake out of this. With his grandmother putting Gemma in the spotlight a short while ago, and after everything with her parents on television, it was understandable that Gemma's emotions would be running high. "I'm taking her home soon."

"Do you want me to come with you? Mom and Dad are dancing, and Gran's having a great time with some old friends, but I don't mind leaving early."

"Thanks, sis, but we'll be fine. Tell the others, will you? I don't want Gemma disturbed once we get home. She's going straight to bed."

"Sure." Bree went to walk away.

"Bree?" Gemma said, stopping his sister. "Er...thanks."

Bree's eyes softened. "You're welcome, Gemma," she said, before hurrying away.

Tate was startled at the pleasure he felt that these two women now had the chance to be friends. He hadn't realized before how unsettled it had made him, having his sister hold a grudge against his wife.

His eyes met Gemma's and a moment of connection passed between them, but turbulence soon rushed into her eyes and she looked away. He was grateful Clive rang on his cell phone right then to say he'd arrived. And, thankfully, no one appeared to notice anything out of the ordinary as they made their way through the foyer and out to the limousine.

Clive held the back door open for them. "Is Gemm—I mean, Mrs. Chandler okay?"

"Yes, but I'm glad you weren't far away."

"So am I," Clive said, looking pleased to have been needed.

Gemma climbed on to the backseat. "I'm fine, thank you, Clive."

They were soon driving off, the partition in front affording them some privacy.

"Tate, I—"

"Ssh. You should rest up." He had things to think about. Serious things.

She turned her head to look out the side window, then just as fast turned back at him. "I won't give up Nathan," she said in a suddenly choked voice.

Everything rolled on its head. He'd been giving her the benefit of the doubt, but perhaps that had been a mistake. His jaw set as he ignored the stricken look in her eyes. "That sounds like a threat to me."

"I don't care what you do to me, Tate. You're not having my son."

He decided pity was overrated. "I won't have *my* son living with another man."

Her face went blank. "Wh-what?"

"If you go to Drake, Nathan stays with me."

She gaped at him. "But…but I don't want to go to Drake. I don't want to go anywhere."

The comment threw him. "You don't?"

"No."

So what was all this about then?

And then he knew. He'd told her he would take Nathan from her if he caught her with Drake again. And he would have done it—if he still believed she wanted the other man.

"Then we're staying married," he told her, getting back to what was important.

Her eyes widened, her mouth dropped open. "We are?"

"Nathan is ours. We stay together." He wasn't about to tell her this just yet, but for the first time their marriage wasn't only about their son. *He* wanted her to stay.

"Oh." She swallowed hard, then released a shaky breath. "Well, that's okay then."

"Yes, Gemma, it is."

They completed the rest of the journey in silence. Peggy had been minding Nathan for the evening, but she was at the front door as soon as the car pulled up, her concern obvious. "A nice cup of tea will do you good," she said, once they were inside.

Tate led Gemma up the stairs and waited until she was bed. Once Peggy had brought up the hot drink and left the room, he moved to leave, too. "I'll be downstairs in the study if you need me. Just call me on the intercom." He took a couple of steps toward the door.

"Tate, about Drake—"

"Just let it be." He didn't want to hear the other man's name right now. He was beginning to realize his best friend wasn't all he appeared to be.

Gemma couldn't describe the joy in her heart as Tate closed the door behind him. He might have left her by herself, but she didn't feel in the slightest alone. How could she feel alone when she would be staying married to the man of her heart *and* keeping the son they had made together? Perhaps even with time and understanding would come love?

Then she remembered Drake Fulton, and her throat convulsed. God, Drake had put all that at risk for his own malicious purposes. He'd made her think she'd lost the two most important people in her life. She couldn't have endured losing Tate again. And thinking about losing custody of Nathan was debilitating.

Yet somehow Tate believed she *hadn't* engineered the meeting with Drake. She didn't understand why, or the reason he seemed to have mellowed. Could it be that he was finally seeing his best friend for the person he was? Or was it more that Tate was learning to trust *her?*

She prayed it was both.

Eleven

The next morning, Tate left Gemma and Nathan still sleeping and went down to the kitchen early. He'd had a restless night, his mind trying to figure out if his best friend had been full of lies all along. Drake had convinced him that Gemma was the one in the wrong, but suddenly Tate could accept she hadn't been a party to that kiss.

Or was it merely that he *wanted* to believe in her? Was her innocence simply more palatable, something that would not only allow him to stay married to her but to sleep with her as well? But if that was so, why couldn't he shake the image of that smug look on Drake's face?

In the kitchen, Peggy passed him a cup of coffee, waited for him to take a couple of sips and then handed him the morning newspaper. "I think you'd better see this, Mr. Chandler."

The headline screamed out at him.

Chandler's Baby?

"What the hell!"

Newlywed Gemma Chandler faints at the Humanitarian Awards Dinner last night...

It went on to describe an eyewitness account of Gemma in a heap on the floor in the corridor.

Does the Chandler family have more than their award to celebrate? Will matriarch Helen Chandler soon have another great-grandchild to show the Australian public?

"Damn them!" Tate threw the newspaper back on the bench after reading a rehash of his recent marriage and the reason behind it.

"I see Drake Fulton was at the dinner, too," Peggy said, indicating the article.

Tate scowled and took another look at the front page. He hadn't taken much notice of the photograph, which showed his family leaving the hotel. Drake walked beside Tate's mother, smiling down at her as if he was enthralled by what she was saying. It was the way Drake smiled at all women. Nothing unusual there.

Tate nodded. "That's right. He turned up late."

A frown appeared on Peggy's face. "I see."

Something made him look harder at his housekeeper. "Why, Peggy?"

She hesitated.

"Peggy, is there something you're not telling me?"

She gave a tiny pause, then, "Did Gemma faint before or after Mr. Fulton turned up?"

It was his turn to frown. "After. Why?"

"Well..."

"Tell me," he said, his tone firm, allowing no argument.

"He telephoned here about two weeks ago and spoke

to Gemma," she said, sending shock through him. "It was the time we were moving her things into your room."

"Go on."

"I heard Gemma tell him that he was never a friend of yours and that one day you'd see him for what he was." She grimaced. "I'm sorry, Mr. Chandler. Perhaps I shouldn't have said anything, but I really like Gemma and I didn't like how upset Mr. Fulton made her. I know this is presumptuous of me, but I have to say it even if I lose my job. I think Gemma's right to be wary of your friend."

Tate felt like his eyes were being pried open. Wide open. Wasn't it around that time Gemma had seemed distracted? It must have been because of Drake's phone call. His blood boiled as he thought about Drake saying something to upset her or, worse, doing something.

"I appreciate you telling me, Peggy. And no, you're not going to lose your job for speaking your mind."

Relief swept over her face. "Thank you."

His grip tightened on the newspaper in his hand. "I'll take this upstairs. I don't want Gemma seeing it."

Peggy's eyes softened. "She's lucky to have you looking out for her, Mr. Chandler."

An odd sensation flowed through his chest. "I'm beginning to think *I'm* the lucky one, Peggy."

And he meant it.

He left the kitchen and went back upstairs. Gemma was on their bed in her nightgown looking gorgeous, playfully tickling Nathan's tummy. He watched the pair of them, loving the moment and the sound of their giggling. His throat squeezed with a deep tenderness.

She looked up and an unusual warmth entered her eyes. "Tate, I didn't see you there."

"You two are having fun. I didn't want to disturb you."

He wanted to extend this moment. Nathan saw him then and tried to get down off the bed. Tate strode forward and swung his son off the mattress and up into his arms. "Hey, buddy," he murmured, cuddling him close. He smelled so...*his*.

Tate's eyes met Gemma's.

Theirs.

In danger of becoming too emotive, he was thankful that Nathan squirmed to get down on the floor. He placed the baby on the carpet just as Gemma said, "You've brought the newspaper."

His head snapped up, not realizing he'd thrown the paper on the bed when he'd picked up Nathan.

She was unfolding it. Her eyes casually flicked over the front page...then went wide. "What's this?"

There was no easy way to say it. "You made the papers last night."

The blood drained from her face as she began to read more. "They're suggesting I'm pregnant."

"Yes."

"But I'm not. I'm on the pill. And I didn't faint because of—"

He didn't want her saying Drake's name. "Would being pregnant again be the end of the world for you?"

"Of course not!" she exclaimed, falling for the diversion. "I'd love another baby someday." A blush spread across her cheeks even as she lifted her chin with a sort of dignity. "But I want it to be something private."

He more than identified with what she was saying. "We're in the public eye now, so we'll be news whatever we do, I'm afraid."

She let out a breath and threw the paper aside as she got out of bed. "I know."

"But that doesn't mean we can't remain private people at home," he said, sharing what his grandfather had once told him. "They don't, and can't, know everything."

She considered the words. "That's true."

"So don't let it—"

"Tate! He's walking!"

"What?" He felt his son grab hold of his leg.

"Nathan walked! It was only a couple of steps from that chair to you, but he did it."

Tate looked down at his son, who was now standing pressed against his trouser leg. A lump rose in his throat.

Gemma crouched down a few feet away and spoke to Nathan. "Darling, walk to Mommy."

Nathan looked across at his mother and hesitated.

"Come on. You can do it, darling. Come to Mommy."

Nathan let go of Tate's leg, wobbled and then took three steps in a rush to his mother, who scooped him up, tears in her eyes, sheer pride written across her face. Tate could feel that lump rise farther in his throat and choke him up. At that moment he knew he'd never give up Gemma or his son. He'd fight to the death for them.

Their son had walked.

Gemma couldn't believe how wonderful it felt to see Nathan take his first steps, and how perfect that Tate had been there to share the special event with her. Not even that invasive article about her being pregnant could dull her excitement.

Their son had walked.

Then, after breakfast, Tate said he was going out but wouldn't be long. It dampened her spirits a little. He'd been quiet while they'd eaten. At times she'd seen tension etched around his mouth, yet she had the feeling it wasn't directed at her.

On his return, he appeared more relaxed, but he still had a hard look on his face. He was angry at someone. Her parents? Surely Tate would tell her if it was something to do with them.

Or could this be about Drake Fulton? Her heart lifted. As far as she knew, no one else had done anything to cause Tate anger. Oh, she did so hope that Tate was finally seeing Drake's true colors.

"Gran's decided she wants to hold an impromptu party tonight," Tate told her now, as she and Nathan sat on the sunroom floor building a tower with wooden blocks.

"Tonight?"

He got down on his haunches, ruffled his son's hair and added a block to the tower. "I think she's feeling bereft that my grandfather isn't around to share the award, and this is her way of keeping busy. She and Bree have been on the phone all morning inviting people."

Gemma remembered how nice Bree had been to her last night. Would it continue? "It's short notice, isn't it?"

"Yes, but it's only for family and close friends. Whoever can make it, really."

Her heart gripped with an insidious fear. She couldn't bring herself to mention Drake. And then she remembered something. "People will be curious…about me, I mean. They'll be speculating that I'm pregnant."

"We can't stop them, but I'll be there with you any-way."

His reassurance meant a lot to her.

"Peggy's agreed to babysit again." He got to his feet. "I'll be in the study for a while. I promised Gran I'd make a couple of calls for her."

He left them to their tower.

At the party that evening at Helen's house, Gemma took a quick look around as they entered the large entryway, grateful not to see any sight of Drake. She was amazed at the number of guests. "Family and close friends, I believe you said," she teased Tate. It was standing room only.

His firm lips quirked with wry humor. "Gran's been around a lot of years. She's made many close friends."

"There's got to be at least sixty people here."

"Eighty, actually," Helen said, coming to welcome them with a kiss on the cheek for both of them. Gemma couldn't help but be relieved she was still in the older woman's favor. She wasn't sure the awards dinner hadn't been a dream.

Or a nightmare, where Drake was concerned.

And then the nightmare arrived.

"How's my favorite grandmother?" Drake said, bestowing a kiss on Helen's lined cheek.

Helen tutted. "If your grandmother was here she'd have something to say about that, young man."

He chuckled, then nodded at Tate, before his gaze slid to Gemma, his practiced smile fading with concern. "I hope you're feeling better now, Gemma. You could have hurt yourself fainting like that last night."

Gemma felt the slightest stiffening in Tate's body and knew he wasn't comfortable with Drake. But surprisingly, she felt Tate's hand squeeze her waist, as if he was trying to bolster her spirits. It gave her the courage to put on a fake smile. "Thankfully, Tate was there for me."

There was a flash of something vicious deep in Drake's eyes, before he turned to Helen with an easy smile. After that, he was all false charm with the other woman and buddy-buddy with Tate, then Darlene and Jonathan joined them, followed by Bree. Tate's sister was friendly to Gemma before she took off again, and eventually Drake moved to another group of people.

A while later, Tate mentioned wanting to talk to a business acquaintance across the room, and Helen waved him off, saying she would look after Gemma. Gemma nodded at him that she would be fine, but she was warmed by his concern about leaving her alone.

After a while, Helen put her hand on Gemma's arm and drew her aside. "Darling, I wonder if you could do me a big favor?"

"Of course, Helen."

"I'm expecting a friend of Nathaniel's to call me at eight. Dougal's old and he's in a home, and if I don't answer the phone he won't call back. Do you think you could go to the study and wait for his call, then come and get me? I don't want to leave my guests just yet."

Gemma was a little confused by the request, especially as Helen seemed to have so many staff helping out tonight, but if that was what she wanted... "Sure. I'd be happy to do that."

"Thank you," Helen said, looking pleased. "I thought you might like a little time to yourself, too. I know it's been stressful for you lately."

That was really nice of her. "Yes, it has."

Helen glanced at her watch. "It's fifteen minutes to eight. The study is down the hall on the right. Just go in there and wait and come get me when Dougal phones."

"Okay." Gemma went to step forward, then stopped. "I'd better tell Tate." She didn't want him worrying if he couldn't find her. Then she saw that Tate had moved away from the business acquaintance and was now talking to Drake. Her heart sank.

"No, I'll do that," Helen said, shooting relief through Gemma. "You go put your feet up. The party won't finish for another couple of hours, and there are plenty of guests who still want to talk to you."

That was enough for Gemma. The thought of everyone asking questions almost had her running for the study.

By the time Tate saw Gemma leave the room, he'd already positioned himself next to Drake. He was in the middle of a discussion with him when his grandmother approached.

As planned.

"Tate, darling," she said, reaching them. "I'm expecting a phone call from Dougal. He's your grandfather's old friend, if you remember. I hope you don't mind, but Gemma's gone to the study to wait for the call for me. I thought she looked a little peaked, so it will do her good to get away from the crowd."

Tate put on a frown and went to move. "I'd better go see how she is."

Helen placed her hand on his arm. "No, don't, darling. She really is okay and just needed a moment to herself. She said for you not to worry. She'll be back in no time." Helen squeezed Drake's arm. "It's so nice to see you here, Drake." Then she walked away.

"Your grandmother's fantastic, Tate."

"She certainly is."

Drake considered him. "Go to Gemma if you want."

"No, Gran's right. It'll do Gemma good to have some time to herself."

He hated using Gemma as bait to lure Drake into showing his hand, but he had to put an end to this for everyone's sake, especially Gemma's. He now believed she had been telling him the truth all along. God, he wasn't sure how he was managing to even talk to his so-called best friend.

Drake's brows drew together. "Maybe Gemma is feeling stressed because I'm here." He paused. "Sorry again that I couldn't get out of coming tonight, man. Your grandmother insisted."

"That's okay. It's all water under the bridge."

Drake's eyes looked more calculating than not. "You seem pretty confident about Gemma now."

With his own eyes wide open, Tate could see that his friend was getting desperate. It was now or never. "I am."

There was a moment of stony silence.

"I guess if Gemma's pregnant..."

Tate knew the other man was fishing, trying to get a handle on how he could best do damage to the marriage. But why? What was this all about? It had to be something damn significant if his friend was trying to do this to him and Gemma.

Could Drake even be behind the newspaper headline this morning about Gemma being pregnant? Hell, could he even have had something to do with the internet pictures? The thought clenched tight and wouldn't let go.

"We're both hoping for more children," Tate said deliberately, hoping to spur the other man into action, knowing he'd hit the mark when he saw Drake's jaw clench. Tate scratched his earlobe, giving his grandmother the signal.

"Tate, can you come here for a minute?" his grand-mother called out to him from where she was holding court with some friends.

Tate looked back at Drake and feigned a wry smile. "I'd better go see what Gran wants."

Drake's answering smile was tight. "Yeah, don't keep the lady waiting."

Tate walked away, but before he'd even reached his grandmother, she gave him a slight nod.

Drake had left the room.

Gemma sat on the leather executive chair behind the large desk and saw the clock ticking toward eight. She had to admit that Helen had done her a favor by asking her to come in here and wait for the phone call. She'd badly needed to get away from Drake's presence, hovering like the snake he was, ready to strike.

She was surprised that Tate didn't seem more upset about it all. Oh, he had that small tightness around his mouth telling her he wasn't happy having Drake here, but he still didn't seem to be accusing her of anything. And that was gratifying, if somewhat confusing.

The opening of the study door broke into her thoughts. The sound of the party rushed in as she saw a tall figure step inside and close the door behind him.

This time she didn't get the man wrong.

Drake.

A sense of déjà vu washed over her.

"So this is where you're hiding?" he mocked, remaining in front of the door, barring her escape.

"This is a private room, Drake," she said, trying not to look like she was frozen in her chair.

He started toward her, "All the better."

"What do you mean?" Her stomach churned. She knew there was a door leading out to the terrace, but the heavy drapes had been pulled across it, and she doubted she'd get to it before him. If only the telephone would ring.

It remained silent.

"You didn't think I would give up, did you?"

"Give up what?"

He stopped right in front of the desk. *"You."*

Her brain stumbled then righted. Was he going to take her at any price? She couldn't let him. Everything she had, everything she loved, was at risk here. She couldn't let him take it all away. Not again.

Somehow she managed to get to her feet and pull back her shoulders, making herself taller, though she wasn't foolish enough to move from behind the desk. If she did, he would attack.

"Why are you doing this, Drake?" she said as calmly as she could. "I never encouraged you."

His eyes narrowed. "Maybe that's the attraction."

In that split second she realized he was used to intimidating her. He wasn't used to her fighting back. She might have disagreed with him on the telephone every time he'd called, but there hadn't been a chance to stand up to him in person. Why, even at the awards dinner last night she'd pleaded with him to let her go.

No more.

"You knew I thought it was Tate I was kissing two years ago," she said, determined to make him accountable.

"Oh, yeah, I knew, Gem."

He was a bully. "Yet you're Tate's best friend. Why would you risk your friendship like this?"

"Am I risking it? I don't think so." He paused, his confidence returning. "You know, it's a pity about your upcoming divorce. Your marriage really was over so quickly. But hey, that's the way with these high-profile marriages."

Inside she gasped, outside she didn't flinch. "What do you mean?"

"Once I make you mine, I'll have to tell Tate how you finally succeeded in seducing me."

She held her ground. "He won't believe you."

He rubbed his chin, cocky and obnoxious. "Oh, I think he will."

"Actually, Drake, I know I won't," Tate growled, pushing the drapes aside and stepping in from the doorway to the terrace.

This time Gemma did gasp out loud.

And so did Drake Fulton.

Twelve

Looking across the room at the other man, Tate had never felt a deeper sense of cold triumph. How had he ever thought Drake was a man of his word?

"What *is* this?" Drake demanded, recovering quickly.

Tate moved farther into the room. "I set you up, you son of a bitch."

"And I helped him," Helen Chandler said, stepping in from the terrace.

Drake winced.

Anger rolled through Tate. "All I want to know is why, Drake?"

Masking his face now, the other man gave a careless shrug. "You took my girlfriend all those years ago, so I decided to take yours."

Tate blinked, then blinked again in disbelief. "Good Lord! You mean *Rachel?* That was back at university."

He shook his head. "And she made a play for me, not the other way around. You said it didn't matter anyway."

Drake's face turned rigid. "I lied. She mattered to me, Tate. Just like Gemma mattered to you. I could tell that, you see. It made my vengeance all the sweeter."

Tate glanced at Gemma and their eyes collided. His heart raced as he saw hope flare in those blue depths. She *wanted* him to care for her.

He did, he promised in return.

His gaze returned to Drake. "You're right about that, Drake. Gemma *does* matter to me," he said out loud. "More than you know." He heard her make a soft sound, but it was Drake's harsher rasp that kept his attention fully focused on the man.

Like a spoiled child, Drake burst out, "I was behind the internet pictures and the newspaper story about her being pregnant."

Rage sliced through Tate. Drake's confession only confirmed what he'd already suspected, but didn't lessen his anger. "I want you out of this house and out of my life. If you ever come near my family again, you'll be sorry."

"Fine with me," Drake snapped. "I achieved what I wanted to do anyway. I split you up for two years. You missed your son's birth and his first year of life." A gloating smile stretched his lips. "That can't be replaced, can it, Tate?"

"Why you—" Tate stepped forward, fist clenched, his chest squeezed so tight that—

His grandmother put her hand on Tate's arm, and he let her stop him. She glared haughtily at Drake. "I'll see you out, Drake. And I suggest you head back overseas as soon as possible and never show your face here again. I'll destroy you if you do." Her tone said she would do what she said. She might be small, but she was a formidable woman. Drake couldn't fail to recognize that.

"Good riddance to you all," he barked, twisting away and stalking out of the room. He almost took the door off its hinges as he slammed the wood shut.

For a few seconds no one moved.

Then Helen went after him, her beautifully aged face easing into a smile as she blew them a kiss before leaving.

And then there were two.

The clock ticked.

Tate's gaze slid back to the woman he loved. Oh, yes, he *loved* Gemma. The knowledge of it had hit him hard when he'd stood outside on the terrace and heard Drake threaten her. The instinct to protect this woman had risen from the very core of him. It had been about more than saving her from harm, more than shielding her from a vengeful, vindictive traitor-of-a-friend. The groundswell of emotion inside him made him want to protect her, to honor her, to share with her the happiest life possible. No one would stop him. Nothing would break them apart. Not again. Never again.

He moved to her, and she was already coming around the desk and flying into his arms. He hugged her tightly, welding her to him. She felt so good, so right. She had to feel something for him, too. Could it be *love?*

"It's over now, darling," he murmured, kissing her eyes, her ears, burying his face in her hair and inhaling the scent of the woman he loved. She was everything to him.

Gemma relished having Tate's arms around her, but she was having trouble believing what had just happened. There had evidently been no phone call expected from

Dougal. Tate had planned this to catch Drake. That meant he finally believed she was innocent.

Thank you, dear Lord.

She leaned back and lovingly looked up at her husband's strong face in wonder. "No, Tate, you're wrong. It's not over."

He frowned, but she could see he wasn't too worried. "It's not?"

Her hands slipped up and framed his face. "It's only just begun, my darling. I love you, Tate Chandler. I love you so very much."

He drew in an unsteady breath. "Oh, God, I love you, too, Gemma. More than life itself."

Their lips and hearts met for timeless minutes. This was love at its finest. It didn't get any better—any more genuine and absolute—than this.

Eventually they eased apart and Tate smiled at her with a love she would cherish forever.

A moment later, deep regret seeped into his eyes. "Forgive me, darling, for all I've put you through. I don't know how I didn't see the truth before. You're a good, kind person, and I don't deserve you at all."

Forgiving him was easy. "There were a lot of things in the way," she excused, knowing that walking through fire had made her appreciate their love. Later, she would tell him how she had loved him from the beginning, but not here, not now.

"Thank you." He kissed her. "Let's make our life a blank sheet of paper from this moment on."

She opened her mouth to agree, then tilted her head at him, her brow wrinkling just a little. "But our pasts have made us who we are, Tate. We've earned our right to happiness. I don't ever want to forget that."

His smile was full of admiration. "See, this is why I

love you so much. You're right, of course. But hey, I don't think we should remember it *every* day."

"Agreed." The sound of laughter erupted in the distance. Clearly Drake hadn't been allowed to spoil the party. "Your grandmother is awesome."

He nodded. "When it comes to protecting her own, she is."

"You didn't do too badly yourself," she teased, forever grateful he had followed his gut instinct. Then she sobered. "I'm sorry I don't have any decent family to share with you."

A part of her would always ache for the love of her parents, but being an adult meant accepting what she couldn't change and living her life to the fullest. Yes, somewhere along the line she'd grown up, too.

"You and Nathan are all the family I need," Tate said, the look in his eyes open and honest. "And let's not forget the two of you have already brought happiness to my family. If you don't believe me, I'm sure my grandmother would be only too happy to confirm that. You brought us back together, Gemma. I'm indebted to you for that."

Gemma buzzed with sheer bliss. "So you've forgiven your mother?"

"We all make mistakes," he said with a self-deprecating smile. "And none more than me."

"She'll be thrilled to have her son back," Gemma said with certainty. "You know, I suspect you couldn't forgive her before because your grandmother couldn't forgive her. I think your loyalties were divided between the two women in your life. In the end, you followed your grandmother's lead. She's a strong woman. Though no less strong than your mother," Gemma was quick to add. "It took guts for Darlene to return and admit she'd made a mistake."

For a moment, a hint of regret filled his expression. "I

know." Then it disappeared and he was back to being the confident man she knew and loved. "Come on. I want to go home and see our son."

His words warmed her heart. "I want another baby with you, Tate."

Something dark flared in his eyes. "So do I. As many as you like."

"I'd like at least three." It was hard to believe this was a possibility now, and that she could share it with the man she loved.

His mouth curved sensually. "Didn't you once say practice makes perfect?"

She went on her toes and kissed his cheek. "I believe I did."

Tate slipped his arm around her shoulders. "Then we'd better get started."

Together they left the study by the terrace door and strolled through the landscaped gardens around the side of the house, heading for the limousine. A night breeze softly traced over their skin, and the brightest of stars twinkled down on them.

Love was definitely in the air.

* * * * *

COMING NEXT MONTH

Available June 14, 2011

#2089 THE PROPOSAL
Brenda Jackson
The Westmorelands

#2090 ACQUIRED: THE CEO'S SMALL-TOWN BRIDE
Catherine Mann
The Takeover

#2091 HER LITTLE SECRET, HIS HIDDEN HEIR
Heidi Betts
Billionaires and Babies

#2092 THE BILLIONAIRE'S BEDSIDE MANNER
Robyn Grady

#2093 AT HIS MAJESTY'S CONVENIENCE
Jennifer Lewis
Royal Rebels

#2094 MEDDLING WITH A MILLIONAIRE
Cat Schield

You can find more information on upcoming
Harlequin® titles, free excerpts and more at
www.HarlequinInsideRomance.com.

REQUEST YOUR FREE BOOKS!
2 FREE NOVELS PLUS 2 FREE GIFTS!

Harlequin® *Desire*

ALWAYS POWERFUL, PASSIONATE AND PROVOCATIVE

YES! Please send me 2 FREE Harlequin Desire® novels and my 2 FREE gifts (gifts are worth about $10). After receiving them, if I don't wish to receive any more books, I can return the shipping statement marked "cancel." If I don't cancel, I will receive 6 brand-new novels every month and be billed just $4.05 per book in the U.S. or $4.74 per book in Canada. That's a saving of at least 15% off the cover price! It's quite a bargain! Shipping and handling is just 50¢ per book in the U.S. and 75¢ per book in Canada.* I understand that accepting the 2 free books and gifts places me under no obligation to buy anything. I can always return a shipment and cancel at any time. Even if I never buy another book, the two free books and gifts are mine to keep forever.

225/326 SDN FC65

Name _____ (PLEASE PRINT) _____

Address _____ Apt. # _____

City _____ State/Prov. _____ Zip/Postal Code _____

Signature (if under 18, a parent or guardian must sign) _____

Mail to the **Reader Service:**

IN U.S.A.: P.O. Box 1867, Buffalo, NY 14240-1867
IN CANADA: P.O. Box 609, Fort Erie, Ontario L2A 5X3

Not valid for current subscribers to Harlequin Desire books.

Want to try two free books from another line?
Call 1-800-873-8635 or visit www.ReaderService.com.

* Terms and prices subject to change without notice. Prices do not include applicable taxes. Sales tax applicable in N.Y. Canadian residents will be charged applicable taxes. Offer not valid in Quebec. This offer is limited to one order per household. All orders subject to credit approval. Credit or debit balances in a customer's account(s) may be offset by any other outstanding balance owed by or to the customer. Please allow 4 to 6 weeks for delivery. Offer available while quantities last.

Your Privacy—The Reader Service is committed to protecting your privacy. Our Privacy Policy is available online at www.ReaderService.com or upon request from the Reader Service.

We make a portion of our mailing list available to reputable third parties that offer products we believe may interest you. If you prefer that we not exchange your name with third parties, or if you wish to clarify or modify your communication preferences, please visit us at www.ReaderService.com/consumerchoice or write to us at Reader Service Preference Service, P.O. Box 9062, Buffalo, NY 14269. Include your complete name and address.

HDES11

"THANKS FOR NOT TURNING ON THE LIGHTS," Tyler said. "I'm a mess."

"Not in my book." Even in low light, Alex had a good view of her yellow shirt plastered to her body. It was all he could do not to reach for her, mud and all. But the next move needed to be hers, not his.

She slicked her wet hair back and squeezed some water out of the ends as she glanced upward. "I like the sound of the rain on a tin roof."

"Me, too."

She met his gaze briefly and looked away. "Where's the sink?"

"At the far end, beyond the last stall."

Tyler's running shoes squished as she walked down the aisle between the rows of stalls. She glanced sideways at Alex. "So how much of a cowboy are you these days? Do you ride the range and stuff?"

"I ride." He liked being able to say that. "Why?"

"Just wondered. Last summer, you were still a city boy. You even told me you weren't the cowboy type, but you're...different now."

He wasn't sure if that was a good thing or a bad thing. Maybe she preferred city boys to cowboys. "How am I different?"

"Well, you dress differently, and your hair's a little longer. Your face seems a little more chiseled, but maybe that's because of your hair. Also, there's something else, something harder to define, an attitude…"

"Are you saying I have an attitude?"

"Not in a bad way. It's more like a quiet confidence."

He was flattered, but still he had to laugh. "I just admitted a while ago that I have all kinds of doubts about this event tomorrow. That doesn't seem like quiet confidence to me."

"This isn't about your job, it's about…your…" She took a deep breath. "It's about your sex appeal, okay? I have no business talking about it, because it will only make me want to do things I shouldn't do." She started toward the end of the barn. "Now, where's that sink? We need to get cleaned up and go back to the house. Dinner is probably ready, and I—"

He spun her around and pulled her into his arms, mud and all. "Let's do those things." Then he kissed her, knowing that she would kiss him back, knowing that this time he would take that kiss where he wanted it to go. And she would let him.

Follow Tyler and Alex's wild adventures in
SHOULD'VE BEEN A COWBOY
Available June 2011 only from Harlequin® Blaze™
wherever books are sold.